FALLEN

from

SIGHT

Monica,
I hope you enjoy!
D R Shoultz

D.R. Shoultz

Author's Note

This is a work of fiction. Names, characters, places, and incidents are the product of the author's imagination or are used fictitiously, and any resemblance to actual persons, living or dead, business establishments, events or locales is entirely coincidental.

Dedication

This book is dedicated to readers of the Mountain Mystery Series, which includes *At the River's Edge, Butcher Road,* and *Fallen from Sight.*

Thank you for your interest. Another mountain mystery will be coming soon!

FALLEN from SIGHT

- The Search Begins -

FLORESCENT LIGHTS burned brightly in the windowless interrogation room. Like a hawk hovering over a field mouse, Detective John Phillips peered down his angular nose at the young suspect seated across the small metal table.

The white-haired veteran of the Parsons Creek Police Department (PCPD) wore a wrinkled dress shirt with his narrow tie pulled loose. Sgt. Mitch Williams was seated beside him in a khaki uniform with a gold badge stuck to his barrel chest, his high and tight haircut adding to his no-nonsense appearance.

"Tell us again," Phillips ordered. "Where and when did you last see Sarah Campbell?"

Ryan Nelson rubbed his face and took a deep breath, his weary eyes showing anger and frustration. The two-hour interview was taking its toll.

"I've already told you. We watched a movie at my place Friday night. I gave her a goodnight kiss on the front porch around midnight, and then she drove away."

"And that was the last time you saw her?" Phillips asked.

"That's right. She wanted to go hiking the next morning, but I had to work."

"Did she say if she had plans to go with anyone else?"

"No. We usually hike alone. Sometimes she brings Patches."

"Her dog?"

"Yeah, her springer spaniel. I found him at her house after she didn't call or come by on Saturday night. He's at my place now."

"How would you describe your relationship with Ms. Campbell? Any recent disagreements or arguments?"

Ryan's jaw clenched as he raked his hand over his thick dark hair.

"We've dated more than a year, and we rarely argue about anything."

"Rarely?" Phillips asked, leaning forward.

"Do you ever have disagreements with your wife, detective?" Ryan asked.

"My wife isn't missing!" Phillips shouted.

Ryan exhaled and leaned back.

"Listen, I want to find Sarah more than anyone. You keep asking the same questions, over and over. I have no reason to hide anything from you or anyone else."

"You were the last one to see Ms. Campbell. You claim to have driven to Boone on Saturday, but no one can verify your whereabouts during the day."

"Stop with the bullshit!" Ryan shouted, twisting in his chair. "I told you I picked up building supplies and then drove straight back to a job site. It only took a couple of hours. You act like I'm some drifter passing through town. I'm the one who reported her missing Saturday night, for crying out loud!"

"Okay. Just relax," Phillips said. "We're trying to make sure we don't overlook anything."

The detective paused, giving the twenty-eight-year-old boyfriend of the missing woman a chance to cool down.

FALLEN from SIGHT

"A hiker found Sarah's grey scarf on the cliff's edge at Jefferson Peak yesterday," Phillips said. "It was clinging to a shrub just below the lookout point. What do you make of this?"

"She must've dropped it," Nelson replied, "or it could have blown off in the wind. Her car was at the base of the trail, so she probably walked to the top. It's a hike we make several times a month."

"Do you ever climb that cliff?"

"We'd never climb Jefferson Peak. It's five hundred feet of slick granite. Besides, she wouldn't go climbing alone."

"Was Ms. Campbell depressed, or are you aware of anyone who'd want her harmed?"

Ryan grimaced, shaking his head. "Everyone likes Sarah. You won't find a more upbeat, kindhearted person in Parsons Creek."

"Didn't she move here from Charlotte a few years ago?"

"That's right. Her real estate company relocated her to sell retirement property up on Jakes Mill Road. I met her while working on the condos up there."

"Did she ever mention any controversy from her past?"

"No, and if you knew her, you'd realize how ridiculous you sound," Nelson replied, standing. "Now, unless you plan to arrest me, I need to get home."

Detective Phillips and Sgt. Williams exchanged glances. Williams shook his head, indicating he had nothing to add.

"That's all for now," Phillips said. "We'll stay in touch."

"I'm sure you will," Nelson replied, turning and stepping from the room.

As the door closed, Sgt. Williams turned to Detective Phillips. "What do you think?" he asked.

3

"Husbands and boyfriends are the most likely suspects, but I think the kid is clean."

"I'm not so sure," Williams replied, frowning.

THE FALL SKY was a brilliant orange as the sun set behind the grey-smoked mountains. Ryan pulled into his driveway not noticing.

The past two days had been the most agonizing of his life. He feared the worst, but held out hope. Initial searches at Jefferson Peak and the base of the cliff had produced nothing. Park rangers and police were to begin again at daylight.

Patches barked wildly as Ryan cracked open the garage door into the house. The eager spaniel ran to him and circled his legs several times before plopping sphinxlike at his feet, staring upward. Ryan glanced at a wall clock. It was 7:15, two hours past the dog's feeding.

Ryan scooped a cupful of dry food from a twenty-pound bag into Patches' bowl. The spaniel's tail whipped the air as Ryan bent down to place the bowl on the floor. While Patches devoured the food, Ryan stepped to the living room and fell into his recliner.

She was here two nights ago, he thought.

He turned to a picture of Sarah on the side table and picked it up. The photo was taken the prior spring at the finish line of a 10K charity run benefitting the local animal shelter. Patches accompanied her during the race.

Even after running the six-plus miles, Sarah appeared as fresh and crisp as that early spring morning. Twenty-seven years old, she could pass for seventeen. She possessed timeless features: warm brown eyes, thick auburn hair, and a calming smile that made strangers like her before she said a word.

Ryan's cellphone chirped in his pocket. He returned the photo to the table, pulled out the phone, and looked down to see a familiar number. It was Sarah's twin sister, Beth.

"Any news?" she asked.

"Nothing. I just came from the police station. Detective Phillips and that bulldog-faced sergeant spent a couple of hours grilling me."

"They think you're a suspect?"

"They're just grasping at straws, like all of us," Ryan said, sighing.

"I've got a bit of good news," Beth said. "I've rounded up about twenty volunteers to search the park tomorrow. Most of them are hiking and climbing friends from Charlotte and a few are from my law office."

"They'll need to be experienced hikers. It's rough terrain around where Sarah disappeared," Ryan replied.

"I'm afraid of what we'll discover," Beth said. "But I have to know where she is."

"I walked the trail from where they found her car to the top this morning, but I found nothing."

"Do you think she fell from the peak?" Beth asked.

"The winds can be fierce up there, but I doubt she fell. Not by accident, anyway."

"I can't believe anyone would hurt her."

"There are crazies everywhere, even up here," Ryan replied, staring across the room at Patches, nosing his bowl, looking for more food.

5

"You don't have to tell me about crazies. Being a paralegal in a criminal law office, I see plenty of them," she added.

"Then you know what I mean."

"I'm glad Mom and Dad aren't here," Beth said, her voice cracking. "This would rip them apart."

"There's still a good chance she's okay," Ryan said. "Maybe she sprained an ankle and was too hurt to hike back to her car. There's no cell service on that side of Jefferson Peak, so she'd have no way to contact anyone."

"I try to think of good outcomes, but it's not like Sarah to disappear like this," Beth said, pacing the floor of her uptown condo. "She and I have talked every night for as long as I can remember. We finish each other's thoughts and sentences. She *has* to be okay. Losing her would be like losing half of myself."

"We'll find her," Ryan said. "She's an experienced hiker and knows these woods as well as anyone."

"My friends and I are caravanning from Charlotte in the morning. If all goes as planned, we'll arrive around nine. Where should we meet?" Beth asked.

"Stay clear of downtown Parsons Creek. The news crews are arriving, and you'll attract attention."

"Where then?"

"There's a ranger station inside Jefferson Park about six miles off Route 421 on Murdock Road. We can spread out and walk toward the base of the peak from there."

"Okay. See you then," Beth replied. "Oh. I almost forgot."

"What's that?"

"One of the guys coming tomorrow is an old flame of Sarah's. His name's Guy Fletcher. They dated her first two years at App State. He insisted on helping."

Ryan frowned.

"She actually dated someone named Guy?" he asked sarcastically.

"Sarah hasn't talked to him in more than seven years. I would know."

"What does he do now?"

"He's a musician. Plays gigs mainly in Charlotte and the Carolina coastal towns. He seemed concerned and was able to get several of his friends to join the search. I hope you're okay with him coming."

"I'm fine with it," he lied. "We all just want to find Sarah. See you in the morning."

- Day 2 -

A CARAVAN OF vehicles turned off Murdock Road, their headlights burning holes through the morning mountain fog. After feeling their way down the gravel lane toward the ranger station, they filed in at the far end of the lot.

Ryan had arrived thirty minutes earlier and sat waiting on the wraparound porch of the rustic log building. Sarah's spaniel was at his side. Spotting Beth in the lead sedan, Ryan rose from an Adirondack chair and stepped quickly down the steps.

He greeted Beth with a hug as the two dozen volunteers began retrieving gear stowed in the rear of each vehicle. Denim jackets and jeans were the attire for the cool autumn morning.

Beth had her auburn hair pulled back in a ponytail. Looking into her brown eyes, it was as if Sarah was standing beside him. Ryan took a deep breath but didn't say anything.

"I'm sorry we're a little late, but the fog slowed us down," Beth said, bending to give Patches a head rub.

"I'm glad you made it safely," Ryan replied. "The rangers and police have already begun searching. The head ranger gave me these maps. Police Chief Adkins recommended we cover the areas marked. He also left instructions to relay to the volunteers. Could you call everyone together?"

"Listen up!" Beth shouted. "This is Ryan Nelson, a close friend of Sarah's and a longtime resident of Parsons Creek. Before we begin searching, he has some instructions from the police department."

FALLEN from SIGHT

The volunteers quieted and gathered close. Ryan leapt onto the bed of a nearby pickup and surveyed the small crowd. The group was mostly men, and all appeared well-equipped with backpacks and hiking gear.

"First of all, thanks for taking time to help search for Sarah. We'll be covering the area from this ranger station up toward the base of Jefferson Peak."

Ryan turned and pointed to the granite summit to the east where the sun was just peering over the edge. Ten square miles of rugged hills, ravines, and woods stretched between where the volunteers stood and the base of the cliff, rising more than five hundred feet toward the clouds.

"The police chief asked that we keep our eyes open for anything that appears out of place. If you find an item that might belong to Sarah, don't touch it. Just tag a nearby tree or shrub and the police will retrieve it. I have rolls of bright yellow tape for tagging.

"We should work in two or three-person teams. Each team will be assigned a section noted on the maps that I'll hand out. Take your time and pay particular attention to the areas around the trails. I know many of you are experienced hikers and climbers, but don't take unnecessary risks. If you see something out of reach, wait for assistance. Cellphone service is poor in this area, so it's unlikely you'll be able to phone for help.

"If you didn't bring sufficient water or food, supplies are inside the ranger station. Help yourself to what you need before we leave.

"Plan to meet back here before seven p.m. Report to a ranger when you return so we'll know who's back and who isn't.

"Are there any questions before I assign search areas to the teams?"

A tall man with dark spiked hair, dressed ready for an REI photo shoot, thrust his hand into the air.

"Yes," Ryan said, pointing toward him.

"Could you assign search areas based on ability? I'm an experienced climber and prepared to go just about anywhere."

Ryan glanced at Beth. She nodded with a sheepish look. It didn't take long for Guy Fletcher to surface.

"All of this territory is pretty rugged, but the areas to the north will be the most challenging," Ryan replied. "I'll save one of these for you if you want."

"Thanks, Bro. I just want to make sure I can help in the best way possible."

"Anything else?" Ryan asked, scanning the volunteers.

"Yeah. Does anyone know what Sarah was wearing when she disappeared?" The question came from a woman standing next to Fletcher.

Ryan paused, thinking of Sarah and what she might have worn. His solemn face silenced the crowd.

"No one saw Sarah on Saturday, the day she disappeared," he finally replied. "She often wore a green sweater and jeans when hiking on cool days, and she would likely have her tan canvas backpack. These items are also missing from her home."

He waited, but there were no more questions.

"Go ahead and pick up your supplies, and then meet me back here to get a map and an assigned area."

Ryan stepped down from the pickup and stood beside Beth as the volunteers dispersed. He looked up to see the self-proclaimed hiking expert approaching.

"Hi. I'm Guy Fletcher," he said, extending his hand. "I'm an old college friend of Sarah's. When I found out she was missing, I had to find some way to help."

"Thanks for coming," Ryan replied. "It's rough terrain out here, and we'll need all the help we can get to find her."

"Is this your dog?" Guy asked, bending to pet Patches.

"No. He belongs to Sarah," Ryan replied. "He'll be with me and Beth today."

"Sarah and I had a dog in college," Guy said, staring down at Patches. "Riley was a shepherd mix, and he was as loveable as the day was long. He was really Sarah's dog, but he stayed at my apartment after she moved in."

Ryan gave Beth a what's-with-this-guy stare.

"I don't know what happened," Guy continued, his tone bordering on sincere. "It was always the three of us back then, and now this."

"Say, if you and your partner are ready," Beth interrupted, "Ryan will give you a map and you can get started."

"Sure. I'm ready," Guy replied. "I'll be teamed with Liz Kline. She's a singer with my band and an outdoor freak like me. She just ran to get a couple bottles of water."

"Here's the section to the north I mentioned," Ryan explained, unfolding the map and pointing to the area. "Beth and I will be covering the section a few hundred yards below you. Call out if you need anything."

"We'll be fine, Bro," Guy said, snatching the map. "See you back here at seven."

Guy stepped toward Jefferson Peak and paused to study the map, waiting for his search partner.

"Bro? What's up with that?" Ryan asked with a smirk.

11

Beth shrugged and smiled. "He's a little intense," she said, "but I think he's well-meaning."

"He's more spooky than intense if you ask me."

As volunteers filed back, Ryan assigned search areas and handed out maps. In less than fifteen minutes, everyone had spread out and headed toward the wooded expanse at the base of Jefferson Peak. Beth and Ryan trailed to the rear with Patches, his nose to the ground, darting from bush to bush.

THE MORNING FOG began to burn off as the sun rose in the southeastern autumn sky.

Ryan and Beth continued to search on and around trails that crisscrossed their assigned section. The paths cut through dense woods, climbed over jagged rocks, and crossed over clear running streams. Patches loped along at their sides as if it was a normal weekend hike. So far, nothing appeared out of the ordinary.

"This seems so futile," Beth said. "Is this an area that Sarah would normally hike?"

"Jefferson Park is over twenty square miles, and we've hiked most of it, including this area," Ryan replied. "But I can't recall her ever coming down here alone."

"Shouldn't we focus on the area where her car was found?"

"The police combed the area from her car to the summit where her scarf was discovered. The trails from Jefferson Peak lead down here, so this is the next logical place she would have come."

"I can't bear to think about her out here alone the past several nights," Beth said, scanning the shadowy, damp surroundings. "Do you think she could survive this long if she was hurt?"

"Sarah always packs water. Even if she was injured and unable to move, she could survive days on a bottle of water," Ryan explained. "It also rained Sunday night. She knows how to gather water from leaves and impressions in rocks."

"How much further before we get to the base of the cliff?"

"We're less than a quarter mile away. The trail will get steeper and rockier the closer we get. Maybe now would be a good time to take a break," Ryan suggested.

"Fine with me," Beth replied. "I just want to make sure we have time to search our area and get back by seven."

"That shouldn't be a problem. It will be quicker going back," Ryan said, unhitching his backpack and setting it on the needle-covered trail. Beth felt for a dry spot on a nearby log before removing her pack and taking a seat.

"Help! We need help!"

The screeching voice of a woman called out in the distance. Patches' ears perked and his head turned toward the screams.

"It came from over there," Ryan said, pointing.

"That's Fletcher's section!" Beth replied, jumping back to her feet.

"Yeah. Let's go."

- 2.1 -

PARSONS CREEK, North Carolina was a town of 9,000 residents. Half were retired. The other half lived off the retirees and tourists. It was a peaceful community set in the rolling hills of the Blue Ridge Mountains.

Catering to out-of-towners, Parsons Creek's three-block-long Main Street was dotted with antique shops, bars, and restaurants. Boone, a larger city and a college town, was less than twenty miles to the southwest, offering whatever Parsons Creek didn't.

Police Chief Roy Adkins, one detective, a sergeant, and a team of five officers kept the peace in the 200-year-old mountain community. In the twenty-plus years Adkins had been in his role, he rarely needed outside assistance and didn't expect he'd require help finding Sarah Campbell.

AS HIS OFFICERS and the park rangers searched the base of Jefferson Peak, Chief Adkins discussed the case with Detective John Phillips in his office.

"I'm still bettin' the girl and her boyfriend had a spat, and she just took off for a few days," Adkins said, leaning back with his feet propped up on his desk.

"And her first stop was Jefferson Peak? I don't think so," Phillips replied. "She'd more likely go visit college friends in Boone or Charlotte."

"Maybe she just wanted to put a scare into the Nelson boy, so she gave her scarf a toss off the summit and then hiked into the park to hide and think. There's plenty of space to do both in that forest."

The lanky detective stood and paced the small office. His tie hung to his belt, swaying as he stepped.

"I hope you're right, Chief, but my gut tells me there's more to this story."

The paunchy police chief dropped his feet to the floor with a thud and leaned forward in his chair.

"Williams thinks the Nelson boy is involved. Do you?" Adkins asked.

"No," Phillips scoffed. "Williams' opinion is tainted by a run-in he had with Nelson a year ago."

"You mean that ticket Nelson fought in court?"

"Yeah. The judge sided with the young carpenter. He ruled the pickup wasn't as overloaded as Williams cited and that Nelson was just doing his job."

"And you think Williams is holding a grudge over *that*?" Adkins asked.

"Williams claims Nelson flipped him off on the way out of court," Phillips replied. "No one else saw it, but if it happened, Williams wouldn't forget something like that. It isn't by accident that he looks like a bulldog."

"So, what is your gut telling you we should do next?" Adkins asked.

"I've been checking missing person reports in the state, but nothing's come up similar to this case. They've been mostly teenagers, and all but a couple of the cases have been open for months."

"Other than Campbell's car and scarf, we don't have much else to go on," Adkins said. "I hope the searchers come up with something today."

"I'm driving out to Rolling Ridge in a bit to talk to Campbell's employer. I spoke with James Rigby on the phone yesterday, but I'd like to go out there and take a look around."

"Good idea," the chief replied. "I'll stay here and hold down the fort. The police radio is our only way to communicate with the search team."

- 2.2 -

ROLLING RIDGE Retirement Village was located three miles north of Parsons Creek and was entering its second phase of development. Upscale cabins, cottages, and townhomes were arranged in clusters among the skyward-reaching pines. The costly dwellings clung to mountain slopes overlooking Parsons Creek in the valley below. A nine-hole executive golf course and a stone-clad clubhouse had been completed two years earlier. Baby boomers migrating from the heat of the south and the chill of the north kept contractors busy. Once completed, Rolling Ridge would be home to nearly one thousand residents.

James Rigby, the owner and developer of the property, arrived at his management office Tuesday morning to find his foreman, Jeb Jones, waiting.

The tall, dark-haired thirty-year-old was dressed in his usual Timberline boots, khaki work pants and green company shirt. Seeing his boss approach, he plucked the cigarette from his narrow face and smashed it in a tray on Rigby's desk.

"I just shooed away a TV reporter from Boone," Jones said. "He was looking for you."

In his fifties, the potbellied Rigby resembled Alfred Hitchcock. He slipped off his tent-sized sport jacket and draped it over his office chair. He then stepped to the coffee brewer awaiting him on his credenza.

"What did the reporter want this time?" Rigby asked, slumping behind his desk with a steaming mug. "Is some tree

17

hugger concerned about what we're doing to the black bear population?"

"No. He was asking about Sarah Campbell. Wanted to know what she did here and the last time we saw her. He stuck a mic in my face and his camera guy started filming."

"What did you say?" Rigby asked, slicking back his thinning hair with one hand and lifting his coffee mug with the other.

"I just said she worked in sales and that we were surprised like everyone about her disappearance."

"Did you say anything else?" he asked sternly.

"No. The guy prodded, but I told him that's all we know. We just hoped she was safe."

Rigby lit a cigarette and blew a plume of smoke toward Jones.

"Go over to the real estate office and get the key to Sarah's desk. Tell Sue that Sarah has information I need about a buyer wanting custom upgrades. I'll be over in a few minutes to look for the customer's file."

"Custom upgrades? Why haven't I heard about this?" Jones asked.

"The guy was sent to me by a friend. He showed up unannounced last Friday, and I drove him around the models myself."

"Then Sarah wouldn't have any information about upgrades," Jones said.

"That's right. I made it up, you bonehead! The cops will come snooping around here soon, and I need to make sure Miss Goody Two Shoes doesn't have anything in her files that might cause past problems to resurface."

"Past problems? Like what?" Jones asked.

"That's no concern of yours. Just get the keys from Sue. I'll be over after I finish my coffee to take a quick look through her desk."

BEST VIEW REALTY, a Charlotte-based firm, was hired by James Rigby to market his retirement community. They began selling homes soon after the first roads were carved into the 3,000-foot-high mountainside.

Sue Evans managed the sales operation. It was a cushy assignment and one Sue owed to Rigby. She and a team of two Realtors marketed the retirement properties. A model cottage, doubling as a real estate office, was located a short walk from Rigby's management building.

Through her open door, Evans looked up to see the awkwardly handsome foreman approaching. Dressed in her usual burnt orange jacket with a brass name tag over the pocket, the forty-something saleswoman stiffened in her chair.

"What brings you here so early?" she asked.

"And a good morning to you, too," Jones replied, smiling.

"Sorry. I'm not myself these days. Can't stop thinking about Sarah."

"Yeah. Everyone's on edge," Jones said. "The vultures are already starting to circle. I had to send a reporter on his way this morning."

"I guess it's to be expected. It's not like someone goes missing every day from Parsons Creek."

"Sorry to bother you, but the boss was wondering if he could get the keys to Sarah's desk. She probably has information on a prospective buyer asking for custom upgrades."

Sue cocked her head.

"I don't know anything about this. Sarah would have told me."

"Rigby said it came up late last Friday. Maybe Sarah didn't have a chance to discuss it with anyone else."

"I don't like the idea of snooping in her desk," Sue said, crossing her arms. "It doesn't seem right with her missing. Can't it wait?"

Jones paused, his eyes darting around the room.

"This is kinda urgent, and we really don't know when to expect Sarah back," he explained.

"Just the same, I prefer we wait. I'll talk to Jim about it later."

Jones shook his head as he turned to leave. "I'll let him know, but he won't be pleased."

"DO I HAVE TO DO everything around here?" Rigby shouted at his young foreman. "The sales department works for me, not the other way around!"

"I told Sue you'd be pissed, but she refused to give me the keys. She said it wouldn't be right to search through Sarah's desk while she was missing."

Rigby's face burned red as his blood pressure soared. He reached into his top drawer for a pill and washed it down with a swig from a nearby water bottle.

"I'll get the damned key and search her desk," Rigby said. "I just need you to do one simple task."

"What's that?"

"Wait ten minutes after I leave, and then call the sales office. Keep Sue on the phone as long as you can."

"What should I say?"

Rigby rolled his eyes.

"Use your imagination. Ask her about closing dates. Warn her of unexpected delays. Hell, make something up."

"Okay. I can handle that."

Rigby slipped on his sport coat, stomped from his office, and headed across the parking lot. Sue Evans was still seated at her desk as he entered.

"Hey, Jim. What can I do for you?"

"I'd really like to see if Sarah has a file on John Brewer, the customer Jeb told you about."

"This must be important," Sue replied. "I was going to call you later."

"A close friend of mine referred him. Brewer stopped by late last week, and Sarah was taking care of him."

"And you want to search through her desk?"

"That's right. It should only take a couple of minutes."

Sue studied Rigby.

"It's not something I'd normally agree to do, but given the situation, I guess we don't have an option," she said.

Sue opened the top drawer of her desk and found the key to Sarah's desk.

"You've piqued my curiosity. I'll go with you," she said, standing and stepping past Rigby into the spacious front lobby.

On the left half of the room, two desks sat side-by-side facing the lobby's center. To the right was a sitting area with a sofa and two upholstered chairs surrounding a coffee table.

Rolling Ridge posters featuring smiling silver-haired residents were positioned throughout.

Sarah's desktop was cleared except for her nameplate and a hinged frame with two photos. A picture of Ryan was on the right, and one of Patches was on the left.

Sue sat behind Sarah's desk and inserted the key as Rigby stood at her side. She pulled open the top center drawer, which contained pens, paperclips, and other office supplies.

There were two large drawers on both sides of the desk. With Rigby standing to her left, Sue pulled open the top left drawer. A hairbrush, hand mirror, makeup kit, box of Kleenex, and other personal effects were strewn across the bottom. Sue stared at the items before looking up at Rigby.

"I still don't feel right about doing this," she said.

"It won't take much longer," Rigby replied. "Go ahead."

Sue pulled open the lower left drawer. Plastic file labels clicked against the bottom of the top drawer as it slid open. The drawer contained hanging folders filled with documents.

Rigby bent at the waist for a closer look, quickly reading the neatly arranged tabs. He scanned the files looking for county inspections, water and sewer reports, or anything that might contain Sarah's notes on those subjects.

"See anything here?" Sue asked.

"No," he replied, glancing at his watch. It had been more than ten minutes since leaving his office.

Sue started to push the drawer shut.

"Wait," he said reaching toward a file labeled *LOG CABINS*. "Let me check this folder."

He pulled the file and casually glanced through the papers inside.

"Nope. Nothing here," he said, placing the file back where he'd found it.

Sue reached for the top right drawer as Rigby moved to the other side of the desk. This drawer was also filled with file folders.

As Rigby scanned the labels, he felt as if he was playing a game of Russian roulette, and that any second he would spot the incriminating files with Sue looking over his shoulder.

Sue looked up at Rigby. He shook his head and she closed the drawer.

"Maybe this was a waste of time," he said as Sue reached for the final drawer.

The phone in Sue's office rang.

"I'll let it roll to voice mail," she said.

"What if it's news about Sarah?"

She paused. "Good point. I'll be right back."

Rigby waited until Sue disappeared into her office before sliding open the final drawer.

He didn't need to search long. The first hanging folder was labeled *COUNTY INSPECTIONS*. Several documents and pages of handwritten notes were inside the folder. Not taking time to read them, he tri-folded the pages and stuffed them in the inside pocket of his sport coat.

Before closing the drawer, Rigby removed the plastic tab from the hanging folder and put it in his pants pocket.

"Didn't Jeb know you were here?" Sue asked, stepping back into the room. "I told him I'd discuss closing schedules later."

Rigby shook his head.

"I didn't find anything in the final drawer," he said. "You can look if you want."

"No. That's okay," Sue replied.

"I guess I'll have to tell Mr. Brewer we lost his cabin specs."

"Surely he'll understand. The whole state knows about Sarah's disappearance," she said.

"Yeah. I guess so. I hope we hear something soon."

Rigby stepped out the door and headed back to his office as Sue watched with her arms crossed.

FALLEN from SIGHT

- 2.3 -

RYAN AND BETH sprinted through the dense forest toward the screams for help as low-hanging limbs slapped at their faces. Patches ran far ahead, barking wildly.

Out of breath, they finally reached the base of Jefferson Peak, where they found Liz Kline with Patches circling at her feet.

"Up there," Liz shouted, pointing up the side of the mountain. "He's not moving."

More than seventy feet above, Guy Fletcher lay motionless on a jagged ledge jutting from the face of Jefferson Peak. A rope stretching from his waist to a climbing peg twenty feet up appeared to be all that was keeping him from tumbling to his death on the rocks below.

"We spotted something clinging to a bush on the face of the cliff," Liz said, her arms trembling. "Guy went to retrieve it, but lost his footing on the way down."

"You were supposed to mark what you found, not retrieve it!" Ryan shouted, still breathing heavily.

"I tried to stop him, but Guy insisted on seeing what it was."

Ryan's eyes scanned from where they stood up to the ledge where Guy lay unconscious. The base of the mountain provided crevices, jutting rocks, and other footholds for climbing, but the area directly beneath Guy was slick and vertical.

"I'll need rope and more climbing pegs," Ryan said.

"Let me check my backpack," Liz replied, scurrying to retrieve the items.

"You can't be thinking of going up there alone," Beth said.

"If I can reach him, I might be able to lower him down."

"I'm going up with you," she insisted.

"There's no room on that ledge," Ryan argued. "Take Patches and see if you can find a ranger."

Beth frowned. "Are you sure?"

"Yeah. It's hard to tell how badly Guy is injured. The rangers have radios and can call for help once I get him down."

She stared at Ryan long enough to determine he wasn't changing his mind.

"This rope's about a hundred feet long. Here are more pitons and a first aid kit," Liz said, holding out the coiled rope and other items for Ryan.

Beth stood motionless as she watched Ryan lift the lengthy nylon rope over his head and across one shoulder. He then clipped the climbing pegs and first aid kit to his belt.

"Go ahead. I'll be fine," he said matter-of-factly before heading toward the base of the cliff.

With Patches at her side, Beth marched back into the woods in the direction of the park rangers.

Ryan lacked climbing gloves, and his hiking boots were not ideal for scaling the granite cliff, but he was able to find foot and handholds to enable his progress. He quickly scaled up the mountainside to the halfway point. Resting with his foot firmly lodged in a crevice, Ryan stared up the final thirty-five feet to the ledge directly above him.

Guy had driven steel pitons into hairline cracks in the granite during his ascent. The loop at the ends of the pegs stuck out two to three inches from the wall of the cliff. There were several pegs between Ryan and the ledge. The pegs, along with cracks and jutting rocks, might provide sufficient support in Ryan's climb upward.

Ryan's pause caused Liz to pace nervously. "Are you okay?" she called.

"Yeah. I'm fine," he replied, not looking down.

Ryan reached his hand toward the first peg and grasped it firmly. As he lifted his foot from the crevice to search for a higher foothold, small rocks fell from the opening and rattled down the mountainside to the base of the cliff.

With his hand gripping the peg, Ryan's free foot slid up the mountain, searching for anything to support his weight. He felt a jagged rock protruding from the granite wall. Resting his foot on it, he took a deep breath.

Ryan repeated the process several times on his ascent. Each time he reached upward to grasp a peg or a narrow crack in the wall, he searched with his feet to find support. Normally, he'd secure a safety line to the pitons as he moved upward, but unsure of Guy's condition, he opted to climb as quickly as possible.

Ryan finally reached the ledge where Guy lay and pulled himself to where he could clearly see the fallen climber. A gash on Guy's head just above his right eye was dripping blood. Other injuries were likely, but only the head wound was visible.

The ledge was barely eighteen inches wide. If not for the rope fastened to Guy's climbing belt and looped through a piton twenty feet above, he would have surely plunged to his death.

The ledge near Guy's head was narrow, but at his feet was a space where Ryan might be able to sit or stand.

Getting onto the ledge would be a risky maneuver. Ryan would have to pull himself up with his arms, releasing his feet from the surface of the cliff. He'd be dangling more than seventy feet above jagged rocks, clinging by his fingertips.

Ryan gripped the ledge with his right hand and tested it. His hold appeared solid. He then reached up with his left hand as his feet released from the mountainside.

Liz gasped, her eyes wide, as Ryan clung by his hands with his legs dangling below the ledge.

Ryan strained to pull himself up and was able to swing his right forearm onto the surface of the ledge. He tried repeatedly to swing his other arm onto the ledge, but each time it slid back, not finding room for a secure hold.

Running out of breath, the muscles in his arms and shoulders burned as he hung from the ledge. His mind raced, searching for a way up or down.

The loose end of the rope that looped through the piton and down to the clasp on Guy's climbing belt lay inches from Ryan's right hand.

Trapped, Ryan's grip on the cliff was weakening. His feet stretched for the side of the mountain, but he was unable to find a foothold. Out of options, Ryan reached his hand for the rope and grabbed it as he slipped backward from the cliff.

Liz's scream echoed off the mountainside and into the woods as she watched Ryan slide backwards from the ledge.

He grasped the rope with both hands and hung on. After falling several feet, the line came tight, yanking Guy's limp body upward. The taut nylon tether slid through Ryan's hands, tearing at his skin before he was able to get a firm hold.

Suddenly, all was still.

Ryan looked up to assess the situation. The lives of both men were at the mercy of a steel peg driven into the mountain just twenty feet above Guy Fletcher, who now floated a foot above the narrow ledge.

Disregarding the searing pain in his hands, Ryan wrapped his legs around the loose end of the rope and reached hand over hand, pulling himself upward. He gritted his teeth with each grasp of the tether, knowing the piton could come loose at any second.

Reaching the ledge, Ryan found room to swing his feet onto the surface. Securely on the ledge and with his weight off the rope, Ryan lowered Guy Fletcher's body back onto the rocky shelf. He then tied the loose rope around his own waist before kneeling to inspect Guy's injuries.

Ryan felt Guy's neck for a pulse. He was alive, but had lost a lot of blood from the laceration on his head and a gash on his right leg.

The blood flow from his leg appeared more severe, so Ryan cut a short section of rope and applied a tourniquet. He then removed the water bottle from Guy's belt and poured the contents on the wound above his eye. He took a gauze dressing from the first aid kit, placed it onto the deep gash, and secured it by wrapping an ACE bandage around Guy's head. Throughout the application of first aid, Guy remained unresponsive.

Exhausted, Ryan sat with his back against the cliff. It was the first time he'd looked down. The thought of lowering Guy down the jagged cliff while unconscious seemed foolhardy. Without a recovery basket or helmet to protect Guy's head, he'd likely sustain more injuries on the descent.

As Ryan was about to rig a harness under Guy's arms, he noticed something that looked like clothing wedged between Guy and a crevice in the cliff. He reached to pull it loose.

It's Sarah's backpack!

He quickly examined it. Other than a few scrapes, the backpack was intact. Inside the main pouch were two granola bars, half a sandwich, a banana, and a water bottle. He unzipped a side pouch to find Sarah's car keys tucked inside.

Ryan slumped back against the wall of the mountain, staring at the backpack. Several scenarios rushed through his head, each adding to his anxiety.

Patches' bark echoed up the mountainside as Beth and two park rangers emerged from the woods. Ryan leaned forward to get a better look.

"Ryan, are you okay?" Beth called.

"Guy's unconscious! He's lost a lot of blood and may have a concussion!" Ryan yelled. "I can lower him if someone can catch him before he reaches the rocks."

"We've radioed for an air ambulance," one ranger yelled, "but we'll need to get him to a clearing."

After securing a harness under Guy's arms, Ryan secured himself to pitons driven into the mountainside and wrapped his blistered palms in gauze bandages. He then began the task of lowering Guy off the cliff. Releasing a foot of rope at a time, it took several minutes for Guy's motionless body to reach the waiting rangers.

After catching his breath, Ryan gathered the rope used to lower Guy and began to rappel down the cliff. Whirling blades of a medical chopper could be heard in the distance as Ryan descended.

Hovering above a clearing, the helicopter crew lowered a recovery basket and then lifted Guy into the aircraft. With the injured man safely inside, the chopper powered skyward and banked to the southwest. Watauga Medical Center was a fifteen-minute flight away.

The aerial activity brought volunteers, rangers, and Parsons Creek police officers to where Beth waited for Ryan to complete his descent.

"You okay?" Beth asked as he planted his feet on solid ground.

He didn't answer. Instead, with a hollow stare, Ryan held out the brown backpack to Beth.

"What's this?" she asked.

"It's Sarah's backpack. Guy must've found it clinging to the side of the cliff. Inside are Sarah's keys and enough food for a short hike."

The ranger looked to Beth and then to Ryan before turning to those gathered. Somberly, he announced, "We need to focus our search along the base of the mountain."

- 2.4 -

DETECTIVE PHILLIPS' unmarked cruiser slowed to a stop in the Rolling Ridge parking lot just as Jeb Jones stepped from the entrance of the management office.

Jones paused, waiting for Phillips to exit, before descending the steps and walking toward the vehicle.

"Hi, Detective. Anything I can help you with?" Jones asked as the lanky detective reached into the back seat for his sport coat.

"Is your boss around?"

"He's inside, but he's pretty busy."

"This shouldn't take long," Phillips said as he slipped on his jacket and approached the building.

"Is this about Sarah Campbell?" Jones asked before Phillips reached the steps.

"Yeah. I talked to Rigby earlier, but I want to see if I can take a look around."

"Are you searching for something specific? Maybe I can save you some time."

"I think it's best that I talk with your boss," Phillips replied. "If I need your help, I'll get back to you."

The detective turned and marched up the steps to the developer's office. Rigby's assistant, Marge Jackson, was seated at her desk in the lobby. The stout middle-aged woman looked up to see the silver-haired detective looming above her.

"Yes, sir. How can I help you?"

FALLEN from SIGHT

"I'm Detective Phillips with PCPD," he said, pointing to the badge on his belt. "I spoke with Mr. Rigby yesterday and told him I'd stop by later. Is he available?"

She took a close look at the detective's badge.

"He has a meeting coming up with a contractor, but I'll see if he can spare a few minutes."

"That would be great."

Ms. Jackson stood and knocked lightly on James Rigby's door before sticking her head inside. She quickly moved back as the door swung open and her boss appeared.

"Detective, I was wondering when you'd stop by," Rigby said, extending his hand. "Please come on in."

The smooth-talking developer pointed to a leather chair. "Have a seat," he said before retreating behind his massive, oak desk.

"I won't take much of your time," Phillips said. "You've already provided a lot of information."

"I'm glad to help any way I can," Rigby said. "Has there been any progress in locating Sarah?"

"Nothing I can report. The investigation's just getting started, which is why I'm here. I'd like to talk with your employees and take a look around."

"Sure. That's not a problem," Rigby replied, "but I don't think anyone has a clue where to find Sarah. If they did, they'd have come forward before now."

"I understand, but sometimes clues are hiding in plain sight," Phillips replied, poker-faced.

Rigby paused, studying the detective.

"Where would you like to start?" Rigby asked.

"I understand Sarah's a Realtor. Could I take a look around her office and talk to her associates?"

"Sure. Sue Evans is the managing broker of Best View Realty. Sarah works for her. The sales office is in the stone cottage just across the parking lot. I don't have time to go with you, but I'll give Sue a call and let her know you're on your way."

Phillips stood. "Thanks."

"And if you need anything else, please let me know."

"You can count on it."

Phillips stepped from the office, thanking Rigby's assistant on his way past.

Outside, Jeb Jones stood at the back of his dark pickup with one of the development's contractors. They were in deep conversation, but stopped when they saw the detective emerge. Phillips exchanged glances with the two men before proceeding across the parking lot toward the sales office.

The front lobby was vacant as Phillips entered. Sue Evans ended a phone conversation in her back office before coming out to greet Phillips.

"You must be Detective Phillips," she said. "I'm Sue Evans."

"I apologize for the short notice, but could I steal a few minutes to ask some questions?" he asked.

"Sure. Tuesdays are slow, but you never know when someone will pop in."

Sue directed Phillips back into her office.

"I've already asked Jim Rigby many of these questions, but I'd like to get your perspective, as well as the views of others working here," Phillips began, taking a small notepad from his coat pocket.

"The sales staff is just me, Sarah, and Lance Baldwin," Sue said. "Sarah and Lance are sales associates who've been with the real estate company for about five years. Lance gets back Saturday. He's been out of town for a few days."

"Have you spoken with him since Sarah disappeared?"

"Sure. I called his cellphone yesterday afternoon to let him know. I didn't want him learning about Sarah in the news. He was shocked."

"How would you describe Sarah's relationship with Lance and her other coworkers?"

"Sarah was...I mean is...one of the most outstanding sales associates I've ever worked with. She gets along great with everyone. She and Lance are competitive, each striving to outsell the other, but it's friendly competition."

"Have you ever noticed any spats or disagreements between her and anyone?"

"Nothing around the office."

"What about with contractors, customers, or other people she comes in contact with?"

Sue looked down, thinking.

"The sales team is always putting pressure on builders to make closing deadlines, and we're often pushing to get last-minute change orders completed. This can create a little tension, but I wouldn't call it fighting. It's just business."

"Can you point to any recent tension between Sarah and the builders?"

Sue hesitated.

"There's always something. I hate to point to one incident and have you think it relates to Sarah's disappearance."

"I've been doing this a long time," Phillips said. "I don't jump to conclusions. Just tell me what you know."

"Well, about a week ago, I had to step into a discussion between Sarah and Johnny Stratford. Johnny owns a cabinet contracting business. His guys were holding up one of Sarah's closings, and he was blaming the delay on Sarah not providing the customer's specs soon enough. The discussion got pretty heated."

"How did it end?"

"I talked to Jeb Jones, Rigby's foreman. He said he'd handle it," Sue replied. "The closing is supposed to be this Friday, but I still don't think the cabinets are completed."

"Any other disagreements you can think of?"

"No, and I really don't believe any of her coworkers had anything to do with Sarah's disappearance."

"I understand. You're probably right."

"Is there anything else I can help you with today?" Sue asked, shifting nervously in her chair.

"Could I take a look around Sarah's workspace? I'd like to look through her desk. I promise to leave everything as I find it."

"I guess that would be okay, but I'd like to be present. There's customer information in her files that we must keep private."

"Not a problem."

Sue retrieved the key from her top drawer and led Detective Phillips to Sarah's desk in the front lobby. Phillips sat behind the desk and accepted the key from Sue.

FALLEN from SIGHT

He unlocked the desk and opened the center top drawer. Finding nothing of interest, he slid it shut.

"Has this desk been locked since Ms. Campbell's disappearance?" Phillips asked as he pulled open the top left drawer.

"Mr. Rigby opened it to look for a customer file this morning, but he didn't find what he wanted," she replied. "Other than that, the desk has been untouched."

Phillips stopped his search and looked up.

"Were you with Rigby when he looked for this file?"

"Yes. We searched together. I stepped away briefly for a phone call, but came right back. The contents were untouched."

"What customer file was Mr. Rigby looking for?"

"Last name was Brewer, but I can't remember the first name. Jim was looking for custom specs that Mr. Brewer requested while working with Sarah late last week."

"Would Sarah normally create a file for a new customer?"

"Yes, usually, but maybe she didn't have time to create one," Sue replied. "She carried a small spiral notebook in her leather purse. She probably logged the information there."

Phillips paused and nodded, seeming to accept the answer.

He continued searching the desk, but found nothing that might explain Sarah's sudden disappearance. He closed the final file drawer, locked the desk, and handed the key back to Sue Evans just as his cellphone beeped.

Phillips pulled the phone from his coat pocket and looked at the caller ID.

"It's Chief Adkins. Can I take this in your office?" he asked.

"Sure," Sue replied.

Phillips hurried toward the office, picking up the call on the way inside.

"Yeah, Chief. What's up?"

"The searchers found Sarah Campbell's backpack this afternoon. Ryan Nelson had to rescue one of the searchers who fell trying to retrieve it. The pack was stuck on a bush one hundred feet up."

"What about Campbell? Any sign of the girl?" Phillips asked.

"They've been searching near where they found the backpack, and so far, nothing," he replied. "Officer Elliott is bringing the pack into the office, and the SBI is sending its CSI team out of Charlotte to dust it for prints."

"I'll be right in," Phillips said. "I'm done out here--for now anyway."

- Day 3 -

HEAVY RAIN PELTED Ryan's bedroom window, the pulsating sound rising with each gust of wind. A flash of lightning followed by a clap of thunder sent Patches leaping from the floor onto the bed. As the rumble echoed off the mountains in the distance, Ryan sat up and turned to the clock on his nightstand. It was 7:35 a.m.

Ryan patted the spaniel's head, the rope burns on his hands causing him to draw back. Every muscle in his body ached from the rescue the day before.

"Good morning, boy," he muttered. "You need to give me a few more minutes."

Ryan flopped back onto the mattress just as his cellphone chirped on the dresser. He sat back up and swung his feet to the floor. Standing, it took him a moment to steady himself before shuffling toward the annoying sound.

"Talk slowly. I'm still half asleep," he said, recognizing Beth's number.

"I'm on my way back to Parsons Creek, but I just pulled into a McDonald's. This rain is awful."

"It's bad here, too. How close are you?"

"About twenty minutes away. I got an early start after no one else showed up."

"I'm free the rest of the week," Ryan said. "I called my foreman last night and told him my hands were in no condition for pounding nails."

"My boss said I could take whatever time I need," Beth said. "I thought I'd stay at Sarah's place for a few days."

"There's not much we can do until this rain clears."

"I talked to Liz Kline last night. She drove to Boone to check on Guy. She said he's in a lot of pain, with scrapes and bruises over most of his body. He's expected to recover from the concussion and the cut on his leg. All in all, he's very lucky."

"And very stupid," Ryan added.

"Common sense was never one of his strong suits."

"I still find it strange that he showed up after all these years," Ryan said. "I've never heard Sarah mention his name even once."

"I don't think you have any reason for concern," Beth replied. "He's just a free spirit and probably considered searching for Sarah another adventure."

"I guess."

"As soon as the rain lets up, I'll come by your place," Beth said.

"Sounds good. In the meantime, I'll call Detective Phillips to get the latest, assuming he'll talk to me."

AFTER DRESSING, Ryan sat at the kitchen table with a glass of OJ and a bowl of cereal. He reached for a banana from a bowl at the center of the table. Peeling the skin back, the fruit was mushy and dark brown, several days past the edible stage. He tossed it into the corner trash can.

Exhaustion allowed him to sleep for the first night since he reported Sarah missing four days ago. Eating and sleeping seemed a waste of time, but he knew he'd need to keep up his strength. He finished the cereal before calling Parsons Creek PD.

"Police Department. This is Jamie."

"It's Ryan Nelson. Can I speak with Detective Phillips?"

"He's in with Chief Adkins. You want him to call you back?"

"Is there anyone else who can give me an update on Sarah Campbell?"

"Sergeant Williams is at his desk. Want me to transfer your call to him?"

"I guess," Ryan winced. "Go ahead."

"Williams here."

"Sergeant, this is Ryan Nelson. I'm calling to get an update on Sarah and find out what Beth and I can be doing to help."

"Listen, Nelson. You and Ms. Campbell can post flyers, call friends, and search the trails out at Jefferson Park, but leave the investigation to PCPD."

"What about the backpack? Were you able to lift any prints?" Ryan asked.

"The backpack is evidence. I'm not at liberty to share what, if anything, was found. Watch the evening news. We release updates to the press every afternoon."

"Beth is Sarah's twin sister, for crying out loud! Surely you can provide updates to her."

"Actually, she's going to get a chance to give *us* some updates. Phillips is calling Ms. Campbell in today to answer some questions."

"Questions? About what?"

"I can only tell you that Guy Fletcher was rather chatty while under sedation last night. He confirmed his semiconscious ramblings this morning when questioned by Boone PD detectives. It seems the Campbell girls have a history of jealous spats."

"Seriously?" Ryan shouted. "You can't possibly consider statements from a groggy, half-witted musician as credible. There's no way Beth knows anything about Sarah's disappearance."

"That's for us to figure out. Tell her she can expect a call from Detective Phillips this morning."

Ryan stuffed the phone into his pocket and stared out the kitchen window at the rain pouring down.

Whatta prick!

Beth's black Infinity pulled into his driveway through the river of water rushing down the street. Ryan ran to open the garage door and guide her inside and out of the downpour.

"Thanks," she said, stepping out. "I've already been drenched twice this morning."

"Come inside. I just made a fresh pot of coffee."

Déjà vu overcame Ryan as Beth walked from the garage into the house. Sarah had made that entrance dozens of times. He desperately wanted the attractive redhead coming in from the rain to be Sarah.

"Can I get you anything else?" Ryan asked as Patches circled Beth.

"No. Coffee is fine."

Ryan poured them each a cup and placed one in front of Beth as they sat.

"Did you call the police department?" she asked.

"Yeah, I talked to Williams. He wasn't very helpful. Told me to watch the news for updates."

"That was it?"

"He did mention something that I should warn you about."

"Yeah, what's that?" she asked, setting her cup on the table and locking eyes with Ryan.

"He said Detective Phillips is gonna call you in for questioning. It has something to do with what Guy Fletcher told the cops. He said you and Sarah had a history of jealous spats. Any idea what that means?"

Beth's face fell slack as she looked down.

"What is it? Is there something I should know?" Ryan asked.

"I was the reason Guy and Sarah broke up in college," she replied.

"What? You've gotta be kidding."

"It was so long ago, and I didn't think it mattered. Guy and I broke up after a few months, but it took a long time for Sarah and me to patch things up."

"What happened?"

"Sarah was always the popular one in school. She made friends easier than me. She was funnier and smarter, so the boys naturally flocked to her. When Guy came onto me, I was shocked, but flattered in a strange way. One thing led to another, and he broke it off with Sarah. Things got ugly between me and her."

"When did you last see Guy?"

"He continued to call me after college. He actually stopped by my apartment a year ago. I told him I had no interest in getting back together."

"Did Sarah know about all of this?" Ryan asked.

"No. Sarah and I cleared the air years ago, and I saw no reason to open old wounds."

"I can't believe you agreed to let Guy join the search party."

"I tried to talk him out of it. He promised to keep to himself and said he was no longer interested in reliving old times. I didn't see a way to stop him, so I agreed."

"It's hard to imagine you and Sarah ever fighting, especially over a twit like Fletcher. I'm surprised Sarah never mentioned any of this to me."

"I thought the Guy Fletcher episode was behind us. I'm sure Sarah did, too."

"Can you think of anything else he could have mentioned to prompt Phillips to call you in for questioning?" he asked.

"No, but it's hard to predict what Guy might say or do. He has an active imagination."

FALLEN from SIGHT

- 3.1 -

CHIEF ADKINS AND DETECTIVE PHILLIPS were wrapping up their meeting in Adkins' office when a knock came at the door.

"Come on in!" the chief shouted.

The door swung open and Sgt. Williams' beefy body filled the doorway.

"I just spoke with Ryan Nelson. He was looking for an update. I told him to watch the evening news," Williams said with a smug grin. "I also told him you were calling in Beth Campbell for questioning."

"That wasn't very smart," Phillips replied. "It'll just give her time to get her story together."

"I wouldn't be surprised if Nelson and the twin sister are behind this whole thing," Williams said.

"Based on what?" Adkins argued. "An accusation like that better have some tangible evidence to back it up."

The police chief's smackdown sent Williams to a neutral corner of the room where he took a seat.

Phillips' cellphone chirped from his coat pocket.

"It's the CSI lab," he announced. "I should take it."

Adkins nodded.

"Phillips here. I'm with Chief Adkins and Sergeant Williams. I'll put you on speaker."

"I'm Mitch Allen with CSI Charlotte. We worked into the early morning on the backpack. There were just a few surfaces smooth enough to lift prints, but we were able to come up with several sets--four in all."

"I would have expected at least three," Phillips said. "Sarah, Ryan Nelson and Guy Fletcher, the man who fell retrieving the backpack. Have you matched any of the prints yet?"

"We haven't had time. It might take another day or two."

"Let us know as soon as you have matches," Phillips said.

"Will do," Allen replied before disconnecting.

Adkins turned to his senior detective.

"What's your read at this point?" he asked.

"We've searched for two days at the base of Jefferson Peak, and other than the scarf and backpack, we've found no sign of Sarah Campbell," Phillips replied.

"So, do you think she was abducted at the summit, and her backpack was tossed over the edge to misdirect our search?" Williams asked.

"Or it fell off during a struggle. I doubt if she would stage her own disappearance. Food and her car keys were in the pack," Phillips said. "It appears she had a day of hiking planned. Besides, what motive could she have for wanting to vanish, leaving her boyfriend and sister behind without a clue?"

"I agree," Williams added. "I think whoever's behind her disappearance is likely to have his or her prints on the backpack."

"I'll give Beth Campbell a call," Phillips said. "It's time we understand how close she and Sarah really are."

- 3.2 -

SUE EVANS ARRIVED LATE TO WORK after dropping off closing documents at her attorney's office. As she pulled into the parking lot, the sun poked through an opening in the dark billowy clouds.

James Rigby was pacing outside his office, waiting for someone to show up for an appointment. He spotted Sue's car and went down the steps to greet her.

"Hi, Sue. I meant to call you yesterday afternoon, but I got tied up," he said. "How did your visit with Detective Phillips go?"

"Fine. I think."

"You think?"

"Yeah. He said he didn't find anything relevant to Sarah's case, but I got the feeling he was suspicious something wasn't right."

"What makes you think that?"

"He asked if anyone had accessed Sarah's desk since she'd gone missing. I said that you and I looked through her desk for a customer file, but we didn't find it."

"That's the truth. Why do you think he's suspicious?"

"He wondered why Sarah didn't have a file on the new customer if she typically keeps files on all her clients."

"We discussed that yesterday," Rigby said irritably. "I told you John Brewer stopped by last Friday without notice. Sarah probably didn't have time to create a file."

47

"That's what I told the detective. I said Sarah often takes notes in a spiral notebook that she keeps in her purse."

"Yeah. That's right," Rigby frowned. "There's nothing suspicious about that."

"I pray they find her safe somewhere," Sue said, "but the more days that pass, the less likely that will be."

Rigby looked up to see his overdue appointment pull into the parking lot in a black Ford F-150 with tinted windows. The Darth Vader-like vehicle parked in front of his office, and a wiry middle-aged man wearing a crooked toupee, dark slacks, and a brightly-colored jacket climbed out.

"Isn't that Fred Warren?" Sue asked.

"Yeah. I hope he has the results from the perc tests. I've been waiting two weeks," Rigby replied.

"Pretty fancy truck. County inspectors must do well," she said. "Maybe I should get out of real estate."

Sue chuckled at her own joke, but Rigby paid no attention.

"We'll talk later. I need to run," he said, heading toward the pickup.

The two men shook hands before Rigby led Warren inside his office.

"You're not going to like my news," Warren said, tossing a folder onto Rigby's desk.

"What do you mean? The test results can't be any worse than phase one."

"Based on these tests, there's no way you can construct high density housing on that section," Warren warned, pulling out the top report from the folder and handing it to Rigby. "Read it for yourself."

FALLEN from SIGHT

"Come on, Fred. It didn't take much for you to look the other way on phase one," Rigby said, scanning down the report.

"Phase one was borderline," Warren replied. "It'll take decades for the sewage from those septic systems to reach downstream creeks and rivers. You and I will be dead and gone before water tests disclose what we did."

"Surely you can fudge a few tests on phase two. How different can the soil be in that area?" Rigby asked.

"No can do, Jim. I tried for weeks, but given the planned density of housing, I couldn't find one sample on that whole slope even close to county and state requirements. I'm afraid your only options are to install a community sewage facility or invest in alternative septic systems."

"You can't be serious! A sewage plant would cost millions, and the alternative septic systems are four times the cost of conventional. Both options price my retirement homes out of the market. You're putting me out of business!"

"I don't know what else to tell you. It is what it is," Warren said, heading toward the door.

"Wait! Fifty K made the problem go away in phase one. How's a hundred K sound for phase two?"

Warren stopped and turned back toward Rigby.

"I don't know," Warren replied. "It's tempting, but what about your whistleblower? I don't think she ever bought our story about the first soil tests being faulty."

"We've destroyed all the original test results, and our whistleblower has somehow disappeared," Rigby scoffed.

"Please tell me you didn't have anything to do with that," Warren said.

"I'm a tough businessman, but I'm no kidnapper," Rigby replied, stepping to his desk to light a cigarette. "Her disappearance is pure serendipity. We just caught a break."

"Make it a hundred and fifty and I'll destroy these test results and start over," he said. "But I have one additional caveat."

"What's that?"

"You reduce the housing density in that section by twenty-five percent. That might buy us time before fish start floating in the James River."

"It's a deal," Rigby said, picking up the file folder and handing it back to Warren. "This time make sure no one gets their hands on this."

- 3.3 -

BETH CHECKED HER WATCH for the tenth time in five minutes as she waited in the Parsons Creek PD interrogation room. She grew angrier and more nervous by the minute.

Down the hall Sgt. Williams and Detective Phillips made final plans for their interview, keeping her waiting.

"How do you want to handle this?" Williams asked.

"I'll lead and start easy," Phillips replied. "At some point, I'll start pressing. I'll be able to tell if she's holding back."

"Then what's my role?"

"Just act tough. She'll be looking to both of us for our reactions," Phillips said.

"That's it?" Williams asked, frowning.

"Yeah. For now."

The men walked down the corridor to the door of the interrogation room. Pausing briefly, Phillips burst into the room with Williams on his hip. Startled, Beth jerked about to face the approaching lawmen.

"Have a seat, Ms. Campbell," Phillips instructed.

The tall detective sat next to Beth, pulling his chair uncomfortably close to hers. Williams sat across the table, arms crossed.

"I hope this doesn't take long. You're wasting valuable time," Beth said defiantly. "My sister's out there somewhere."

"Are you close to your sister?" Phillips asked.

"Of course. She's my best friend and the only family I have."

"Have you always been close?"

"Sure."

"Did you ever fight about anything? Like over boyfriends?"

"Listen. I know you talked with Guy Fletcher, and he probably told you about breaking up with Sarah to date me."

"Tell me about it."

"That was more than seven years ago. My sister and I've put all that behind us. Neither of us have feelings for Guy Fletcher."

"Did you ever say that you wish you weren't a twin? And that your life would be easier with Sarah gone?"

Williams leaned in as Phillips posed the questions. Beth looked at the jowl-faced sergeant and then back to Phillips.

"I may have said something like that, but it was long ago, and I obviously didn't mean it."

"Before seeing Guy Fletcher this week, when was the last time you talked to him?"

"About a year ago, I guess."

"Did you talk about Sarah's relationship with Ryan Nelson at that time?"

Beth's eyes widened. "What did Guy tell you?"

"Just answer the question, Ms. Campbell. Did you discuss Ryan Nelson the last time you talked to Mr. Fletcher?"

"Yeah, I think so. I mentioned Sarah was in a new relationship, and we briefly discussed Ryan."

"Did you say Ryan was hot, and if Sarah ever broke up with him, you'd give Ryan a call?"

"I was just trying to get Guy to quick calling me!"

"So you told him that you were looking for someone like Ryan?"

"That's right, and it worked. Guy didn't call again until this past Sunday when he volunteered to search for Sarah."

"Where were you last Saturday?" Phillips asked.

"I was home most of the day. I spent the day cleaning and getting ready for a business trip that I ended up cancelling."

"Did Sarah call you the night before?"

"Yeah. I told you that earlier."

"What did you discuss?"

"She asked if I wanted to go hiking the following morning. I told her I had to get my condo cleaned."

Phillips moved his chair closer. Beth pulled back.

"So, you knew where she would be Saturday morning?" he asked.

"Yeah. I knew. So what?"

"Did you also know your fingerprints would be on her backpack when it was found?"

"What are you talking about?"

"Did you and Ryan make plans to find the backpack before anyone else so your fingerprints could be explained?"

"You guys are crazy!"

"Didn't Ryan immediately hand you the backpack after he found it?"

"Listen! Our hopes were to find Sarah, just like everyone else at Jefferson Peak yesterday. Simple as that!"

"Several calls between you and Ryan were placed days before Sarah disappeared. How do you explain that?"

Phillips' tone hardened. He was no longer asking questions. His voice implied guilt.

"You traced my calls?" she asked, her voice cracking for the first time.

"What was the subject of all these conversations?" Phillips asked firmly.

"Our birthday is coming up. Ryan and I were discussing gift ideas for Sarah."

Her eyes began to pool and a tear escaped down her right cheek.

"I love my sister. Your questions are cruel," she cried, covering her face with both hands. "Get me out of here. I need to find Sarah."

Phillips looked to Sgt. Williams and then back to Beth.

"Can I see your driver's license?" Phillips asked.

Beth reached into her purse and retrieved her wallet. She pulled her license from its sleeve and tossed it on the table toward Phillips.

The detective picked up the license and squinted at the birthdate under the photo. He turned to Williams and shook his head before handing the license back to Beth.

"You're free to go," Phillips said.

Beth gathered her purse and fled from the room.

"Alligator tears," Williams said. "And her boyfriend is waiting for her in the lobby."

"We have no other evidence of them being together prior to Sarah's disappearance," Phillips argued. "The phone calls were all we had. For now, it's a dead end."

Ryan looked up from his seat in the lobby as Beth approached. Her eyes were moist and red.

"What happened in there? Are you okay?" he asked, reaching out to comfort her.

Beth rejected his embrace and wiped the tears from her face.

"Let's get out of here. They have no clue what happened to Sarah."

Still shaken, Beth walked beside Ryan across the parking lot to his waiting Ford Bronco.

"Those morons actually believe that you and I are behind Sarah's disappearance."

"Based on what?" Ryan asked.

"Guy told Phillips I wanted Sarah outta the way so I could have you to myself."

"Why would Guy say that? Surely he doesn't believe you'd hurt Sarah."

"Guy lives in a world that only he understands. He knows Sarah and I have moved on, but he can't seem to let go," Beth explained.

"Do you think he's dangerous?"

"No. I don't think so. He's never threatened me or Sarah. He used to smoke a little pot, but he was a happy stoner. It never made him aggressive."

"Should I go talk with him? I'm sure I could get his head straightened out."

"No. It would only give him the attention he wants," Beth replied. "I think it's best to ignore him."

Ryan unlocked his SUV and sat behind the wheel as Beth slipped into the passenger seat.

"What next?" she asked.

"I'm beginning to think finding Sarah is going to be up to you and me," Ryan replied. "The cops are focused on us, and the media is treating her disappearance as a runaway case."

"Searching Jefferson Park seems overwhelming," Beth said. "And since Sarah's backpack was recovered with no sign of her, I don't know what to think."

"If the prints from the backpack had identified a real suspect, Phillips and Williams wouldn't be so focused on us," Ryan said.

"So, what should we be doing?"

"Let's go back to square one and start by searching where Sarah's car was found," Ryan replied.

"That area's been searched several times already," Beth argued. "What do you expect to find?"

"I don't know, but I just don't have a better idea."

- 3.4 -

THE ROADSIDE PULL-OFF where Sarah's car was found was empty when Beth and Ryan arrived. A thin fog hovered following the morning rain, casting an eeriness to the last location where anyone could place Sarah.

Ryan had stopped at home to pick up Patches. The spaniel leapt from the SUV and circled the open area as Beth and Ryan stood staring at the space where Sarah's car was found.

"She loves Jefferson Peak," Ryan said. "We'd just come here two weeks ago."

"Where would she have gone after parking?" Beth asked.

"Probably up the trail to the peak to watch the sunrise, and then she'd likely take one of three trails down to the valley."

"Is there one trail she preferred?" Beth asked.

"The Sunrise Trail is the most challenging and has the best views," Ryan replied. "It's also not a good trail to take dogs, so it might explain why she left Patches at home."

"Let's start there then," Beth suggested.

"We can go a little way, but I'll have to take Patches home if we want to hike all the way down," Ryan replied.

"Let's go as far as we can."

They started up the trail toward Jefferson Peak with Patches running ahead, nose to the ground, darting back and forth. As they reached the peak, Patches scampered into bushes beside the trail and began barking like a hound on a fox scent.

"Must be a rabbit," Ryan said, as he and Beth carefully searched the area.

A moment later, the liver-spotted spaniel came trotting back with a sturdy stick in his mouth.

"Not now, boy," Ryan said, continuing to scan the area.

Patches dropped the stick at Ryan's feet and playfully backed off, looking up at him. Ryan ignored the spaniel and walked away. Patches snatched the stick and followed him, dropping it at his feet again.

"Okay, boy," Ryan said, "but only once."

Ryan bent to pick up the stick. Before tossing it, he looked down and saw what he thought was sap or a drop of mud on its tip. Looking closer, he noticed thin filaments, and what he thought was sap now looked more like dried blood.

"Beth! Come here!"

She hurried to see what Ryan had found.

"Look at this," he said, holding the gnarly stick closer. "Doesn't this look like blood and strands of hair?"

Beth gasped and clutched her arms to her chest.

"Patches found it in those bushes," Ryan said, pointing to the clump of mountain laurel behind them.

"Oh my God!"

"We have to take it to the police. They can verify whether this is Sarah's blood and hair."

Beth's eyes welled with tears, but she quickly brushed them aside with her hand.

"Don't jump to conclusions," Ryan said. "Sarah's tough. If she was taken from here, she could still be fine."

"Phillips and Williams are going to think we knew where to find this," Beth said. "They already believe we're suspects."

"We can't hide it," Ryan replied. "We'd be guilty of concealing evidence. Come on. Let's take a quick look around where Patches found this, and then head back to town."

DETECTIVE PHILLIPS accepted the evidence with judging eyes, first studying the thick branch and then Beth and Ryan.

"How is it that you could find this when Parsons Creek PD and the SBI forensic team didn't?"

"Patches found it well off the trail among thick bushes. He must've picked up Sarah's scent."

"Can you provide samples of Sarah's hair, maybe from a hairbrush?" Phillips asked.

"Sure," Beth replied.

"It'll take twenty-four hours to match whatever's on this stick to Sarah's hair and blood."

- Day 4 -

IT WAS EARLY MORNING when Ryan drove to meet Beth at Sarah's house. Ever since Patches found the stick at Jefferson Peak, all he could think about was Sarah being injured and alone. He pulled into the driveway of the small brick home not remembering any of the three-mile drive.

"Who'd want to hurt her?" Beth asked as they took seats at the kitchen table.

"I can't think of anyone," Ryan replied. "She isn't afraid to speak her mind, but I can't imagine she'd upset anyone to the point of wanting to harm her."

"Real estate sales can be a dog-eat-dog business," Beth said. "Do you suppose it was someone at work?"

"I've worked on homes at Rolling Ridge and met the folks in the real estate and management offices. They don't strike me as capable of violence."

"Maybe she had an argument with one of her clients," Beth suggested.

"Not Sarah. She believes the customer is always right. She'd be more likely to piss off one of the contractors."

"What do you mean?"

"She's pretty tough on builders," Ryan replied. "Once a house is under contract, she makes damned sure they live up to the closing date."

"That just sounds like good business to me," Beth said.

"Yeah. I guess. But being a carpenter, I can understand their point of view, too. A lot of times things beyond your control can cause delays—bad weather, shortage of supplies, hunting season."

"Hunting season? Be serious," Beth said.

"I am. Finding a good subcontractor in the mountains during deer hunting season is nearly impossible. They're all up in deer stands waiting for a five-point buck to pass by."

"Did she ever mention a specific builder she argued with?"

"No. In the end, she usually gets her way," Ryan replied.

"Let's go out to Rolling Ridge and ask around," Beth suggested. "It'll probably upset Detective Phillips, but it's better than just sitting here."

- 4.1 -

DETECTIVE PHILLIPS had just poured his second cup of coffee when his desk phone rang.

"Parsons Creek PD. This is Phillips."

"Detective, this is Jim Parker out at the Jefferson Park Ranger Station. I think you'd better get out here ASAP."

"What's up?"

"Looks like a coyote dragged part of a decomposed carcass into our parking lot last night."

"That sounds like something you guys can handle," Phillips scoffed.

"I don't think so. This carcass is wearing shoes."

"Shoes?"

"It's the lower part of a human body. What's left of it, anyway."

"Don't let anyone near it. I'll be right there!"

IT TOOK LESS THAN twenty minutes for Phillips to round up Coroner Smith and two patrolmen and drive to the ranger station.

The rangers had roped off a ten-foot-square grassy area at the far end of the parking lot and covered the human remains with a green canvas tarp. Jim Parker and another ranger stood, arms crossed, with their backs to the tarp.

Phillips and Dr. Smith stepped from Phillips' cruiser and approached the rangers. The patrolmen following them parked their squad car at the entrance of the lot to block traffic.

FALLEN from SIGHT

"In my twenty years as a ranger, I've never seen anything this grisly," Parker said.

Phillips and Dr. Smith didn't respond. Instead they stepped under the rope up to the tarp. The coroner's aging knees cracked as he bent down and pulled the cover back. The doctor jerked his head away from the stench before being able to focus on what was beneath.

The decomposed hips and legs of what appeared to be a female lay contorted on the grass. Getting a close look over Smith's shoulder, Phillips' stomach wrenched. He covered his nose with his hand and swallowed hard to avoid losing his breakfast.

Dr. Smith stood and looked down at the mangled body parts.

"It's definitely human. Genital region is mostly gone, but the size of the feet and the style of shoes indicate it's a young female. The coyotes have made it difficult, if not impossible, to estimate cause or time of death."

"Could it be the missing Campbell girl?" Phillips asked.

"I can't rule it out," Smith replied. "I'll take a few pictures and then bag up the remains. I'll be able to tell more back at my lab."

"I'll call Frank Willis," Phillips said. "His bloodhounds might be able to follow the scent back to the rest of the body, assuming it's still out there."

"It's worth a shot," Parker said. "But coyotes and buzzards don't usually leave much."

"Is anyone else aware of what you found this morning?" Phillips asked.

Both rangers shook their heads.

"Good. Keep this quiet for now," Phillips ordered. "And Doc, could you do me a favor?"

"Yeah, what's that?"

"Take a couple close-ups of the shoes and send them to my phone."

After photographing the partial body, the coroner loaded the remains into a blue body bag and zipped it shut. With the help of one of the rangers, Smith carried the bag to the open trunk of Detective Phillips' cruiser.

"The patrolmen will stay here and wait for Willis and his bloodhounds," Phillips told the park rangers. "Let me know if you hear or see anything else unusual."

"Sure thing," Parker replied.

PHILLIPS AND DR. SMITH were silent during the drive back to Parsons Creek. With eyes fixed on the road ahead, they considered what could have led to the death of the woman whose remains lay in the trunk.

"They don't look like hiking boots," Phillips blurted, breaking the silence.

"What's that?" Smith asked.

"The shoes on the body. They didn't look like hiking boots."

"No, I guess not," the coroner replied. "They look more like tennis or casual shoes."

"The missing Campbell girl was going hiking. Those shoes don't look like something you'd wear to hike over rocks and tree roots," Phillips said.

"I agree."

Minutes later, as they reached the coroner's office, Phillips' cellphone rang. It was Chief Adkins.

"What's up?" Phillips asked.

"I just heard from the SBI lab," Adkins replied. "The hair on the stick matches the Campbell girl's sample. The tests on the blood are incomplete, but I'd be surprised if it didn't also match."

"We just reached the coroner's office. The remains found out at Jefferson Park are female. No way to tell if it's Sarah Campbell, but Doc Smith says he'll get tissue samples to the SBI lab ASAP."

"What does your gut tell you?" Adkins asked. "Do you think it's the Campbell girl?"

"My gut's in a knot. I don't know what it tells me."

- 4.2 -

RYAN AND BETH pulled into the Rolling Ridge parking lot, slowly passed the management building, and cruised to a stop in front of the sales cottage.

Jeb Jones had just finished his morning update with James Rigby and was stepping out the entrance. Seeing Ryan's SUV, Jones spun on his heels and barged back into his boss's office.

"Ryan Nelson is headed to the sales office," he shouted, "and it looks like he's with Sarah Campbell's sister!"

Rigby jerked his head up from what he was reading.

"What are you so upset about?"

"Phillips has already spoken to everyone. What could these two want?" Jones asked.

"I heard Sarah's sister was leading the search party out at Jefferson Park," Rigby replied. "She's probably curious, and wanting to look around for herself."

"Yeah, I guess so."

"But I do wonder what the Nelson boy knows," Rigby said to himself with a faraway look.

"Knows? About what?" Jones asked.

"Never mind. Just get back to work. I'll handle this."

SUE EVANS' OFFICE DOOR was cracked open. Ryan knocked and stuck his head inside.

"Sorry to show up unannounced, but we're here to ask a few questions about Sarah."

Sue looked up and smiled, seeming to recognize Ryan and Beth.

"Sure, come on in," she said as she stood.

"I'm…"

"Ryan Nelson," Sue interrupted. "We've met before. And you must be Sarah's sister."

Sue reached out to shake their hands.

"I'm terribly sorry about Sarah's disappearance. Have you heard anything new?"

Beth and Ryan exchanged nervous glances. They'd agreed not to discuss what Patches had found at Jefferson Peak.

"No. Not really," Ryan replied. "That's why we're here. We're trying to learn as much as we can from those who know Sarah best."

"I've already spoken with Detective Phillips and told him what I know. It wasn't much, I'm afraid."

"Can we just ask a few questions?" Beth asked.

"Sure. I'm glad to help any way I can. Please sit down."

"Did Sarah get along with all her coworkers?" Ryan began.

"Yes, of course. She had some disagreements, but they were at a business level. Nothing personal," Sue replied.

"Anyone in particular she butted heads with?" Beth asked.

"Not really. Her disagreements were mainly with contractors who were behind on their work."

"Since Sarah disappeared, have any of her coworkers been acting strangely?" Ryan asked.

"Acting strangely? In what way?"

"Differently, nervously, or maybe coming around more than usual," Ryan explained.

"I think everyone's nervous about Sarah," Sue said. "We all hope she's found safe, but I can't think of anyone who's acting differently."

"Well, if you think of anything after we leave, I'd appreciate a call. Here's my business card."

Sue glanced at the card.

"Yes. I'll let you know," she said. "I'll pray you find your sister soon."

"Thank you," Beth replied, her smile reserved.

"Do you suppose Mr. Rigby would have time to meet with us?" Ryan asked. "I met him some time ago when I did work on his condos."

"He's in. Let me give him a call," Sue offered.

Beth and Ryan moved to the outer office and stood next to Sarah's desk while Sue placed the call. The desk was cleared other than photos of Ryan and Patches displayed in a hinged silver frame.

Beth picked up the photos and studied them, unable to hold back tears.

"You know how much she loves you," Beth said, placing the pictures back on the desk.

"Yes, I do. And we're going to find her."

Sue appeared in her doorway, and Beth quickly composed herself.

"Jim said he'd be glad to see you."

"Thanks. I know the way to his office," Ryan replied.

Beth and Ryan stepped outside and headed across the parking lot toward the management office.

"What are you going to ask him?" Beth asked. "I hear he's a real hard-ass."

"I expect he'll cooperate. I think Sarah knows him pretty well, so I'm sure he's concerned. I just want to see what he knows and try to read his reactions."

Rigby was waiting for Ryan and Beth in the lobby outside his office.

"Hello, Mr. Rigby. This is Sarah's sister, Beth."

"Please call me Jim, and I'm glad to help if I can. Come inside and have a seat," Rigby said, extending his arm toward his office.

"Beth and I are meeting with people who know Sarah, hoping we find some clue as to where she is," Ryan said.

"I'm sure Sue told you that Detective Phillips already met with us," Rigby replied. "I don't think he learned much."

"Yeah, but we know Sarah better than Detective Phillips does, so we might be able to pick up something that he couldn't."

"I guess that's possible. So, how can I help?"

"What was your first thought when you heard Sarah was missing?" Ryan asked.

Rigby paused.

"I guess my first reaction was concern," Rigby replied, "and that I hoped she'd just been called away and didn't have time to tell anyone."

"I know Sarah can be opinionated and maybe even a little pushy," Ryan said. "As far as you know, has she pushed anyone too far?"

He smiled at Ryan's observation.

"Sarah was very outspoken, but I think everyone understood she was well-intentioned and interested in making Rolling Ridge successful."

"Yes. She's focused on doing her part to grow Rolling Ridge," Ryan said. "She was devastated when she learned about the soil tests. She thought it was the end of her job."

Rigby's head cocked back. "She discussed that with you?"

"Yeah. There isn't much we don't talk about. You can imagine how pleased she was when she learned the initial tests were faulty."

"Yes, we all were pleased," Rigby said.

"Is there anyone else at Rolling Ridge you'd recommend we talk to? Anyone who might know something?" Beth asked.

"Sue Evans would be my only recommendation, but you've already met with her."

Ryan waited for Rigby to offer more, but he sat silently.

"Please give me a call if you think of anything else," Ryan said, handing Rigby a business card.

"I sure will," he replied, standing.

Beth and Ryan stood and stepped toward the office door.

"Thanks again," Ryan called back.

They walked quietly to Ryan's Bronco and took their seats inside.

"What did you think?" Beth asked.

"I'm not sure, but did you see his face when I mentioned the soil tests?"

"He did seem a little on edge," Beth agreed.

"I think we need to keep an eye on Mr. Rigby."

As Ryan pulled out of the Rolling Ridge parking lot, his cellphone chirped.

"Can you get that?" he asked Beth.

She grabbed the phone off the center console.

"This is Beth Campbell."

"Ms. Campbell, this is Detective Phillips. I was wondering if you and Mr. Nelson would stop by the police station this afternoon."

Ryan overheard Phillips' request and nodded.

"Sure. We're heading that way now. Can you say what this is about?"

"There's something you need to see. I really can't say more on the phone."

"What about the tests on the stick we found? Anything back yet?"

"We'll discuss that when you come in."

- 4.3 -

THEIR RECENT VISITS to the Parsons Creek Police Department were spent in the suffocating confines of the interrogation room. Neither Ryan nor Beth looked forward to a return trip so soon, but they were curious as to what Detective Phillips had to show them.

As they entered the police station, solemn faces in the lobby turned their direction only to quickly look away after making eye contact. Down the corridor, Detective Phillips stepped from a conference room to greet them, his expression more reserved than usual.

"I've got a bad feeling about this," Ryan whispered as the detective approached.

"I'm glad you could come in so quickly," Phillips said. "Please join me and Sergeant Williams in here."

He directed Ryan and Beth toward a conference room where Williams was seated. He looked up and nodded but didn't bother to stand. The sergeant's bulldog face had lost its bite.

"There's no easy way to present this," Phillips began as Beth and Ryan took seats across from them. "The rangers at Jefferson Park discovered the body of a woman early this morning."

"Not Sarah!" Beth gasped, rising from her chair.

"We're not sure," Phillips quickly replied. "It's why we asked you here. The only identifiable items on the body are the victim's shoes. We want to know if you recognize them."

"I don't know if I can do this," Beth said, turning to Ryan.

"We've cropped the photos so all that's visible are the shoes. You'll not be able to see the victim," Phillips said.

Ryan looked to Beth, then back to Phillips, as he took a deep breath.

"It's okay, Detective. Go ahead," he said.

Ryan reached for Beth's hand as Phillips opened a manila folder and pulled out two photos. He spun them around to face the couple.

Ryan exhaled and slumped back in his chair as Beth dropped her face into her hands. Phillips and Williams sat silently, waiting for confirmation.

"Those aren't Sarah's shoes," Ryan said. "That can't be Sarah."

"Are you sure?" Williams asked.

"I'm positive," Ryan replied.

"She doesn't own anything like that," Beth added.

Phillips stuffed the photos back into the folder.

"How did this woman die?" Ryan asked.

"We don't know. The coroner hasn't released his report."

"Where was she found?" Beth asked.

"I'd rather not give you the details, other than to say the body was discovered by park rangers early today. We have officers searching for more evidence in the area."

"What about the SBI lab tests on the stick we found?" Ryan asked. "You said you'd let us know today."

"The blood and DNA tests aren't complete," Phillips replied, "but the strands of hair do match the samples you provided."

Ryan and Beth had prepared for the possibility the hair was Sarah's, but hearing the confirmation sent them into each other's arms.

The relief of knowing the dead woman wasn't Sarah was short-lived. It now appeared Sarah had been assaulted and her whereabouts were still unknown. Ryan and Beth separated, took deep breaths, and sat quietly for a long moment.

"This is a lot to absorb," Ryan said. "Do you have any leads?"

"The details of the case will be kept confidential during the investigation," Williams said. "Once we're able to make an arrest, you'll know along with everyone else."

Ryan bristled, sitting erect, leaning toward Williams.

"We're her family!" he shouted. "We're not going to jeopardize your investigation. We want to help."

"If we need your assistance, we'll call," Williams said.

Beth stood, her expression quickly morphing from sadness to anger. She glared down at Williams and Phillips.

"Let's go, Ryan. We're wasting our time here."

Detective Phillips waited until they left the room before turning to Williams.

"You need to lighten up on them. It's low odds they're involved in either case."

"Based on what?" Williams challenged.

"After doing this for more than twenty years, I think I can read people pretty well. They're bringing us clues. They're not hiding anything."

"I'm not so sure. Maybe they're first to find the evidence because they know where it is," Williams countered. "The first fireman to a fire might have set it."

"You're way off on this, Sergeant."

FALLEN from SIGHT

The lawmen engaged in a brief tug-of-war with their eyes before Phillips stood.

"We can't spend all afternoon in here. We have a missing woman to find and a corpse to identify."

- Day 5 -

AFTER TALKING PAST MIDNIGHT on Ryan's deck, he convinced Beth to stay in his guest room for the evening, or for as long as she wanted. She agreed that she'd sleep better with him and Patches close by.

The next morning Beth awoke to the sound of a TV blaring in the living room. It took her a few moments to get her bearings before wandering down the hall, rubbing her eyes, her hair knotted atop her head. She wore a pair of Ryan's gym shorts and a tee shirt with *Nelson Contracting* printed across the front.

"We don't need to worry about getting enough publicity now," Ryan said, sitting on the edge of a living room chair. "Parsons Creek is all over the cable news channels."

"What are they reporting?" Beth asked.

"Apparently our friends at the police department have disclosed foul play in Sarah's disappearance. Plus, they've announced the body of a second female found in Jefferson Park yesterday morning."

"Phillips will be getting all the support he can handle now," Beth said. "I've seen the level of scrutiny that will be coming from the SBI and state authorities."

"I did some checking last night online," Ryan said. "In the past five years, Parsons Creek PD has investigated only a handful of felonies--mainly burglaries, drug busts, and domestic abuse. One murder occurred three years ago, but the husband confessed to killing his wife two days later. They've never led investigations like the two they face now."

"I hope the other case doesn't detract attention from finding Sarah," Beth said.

"I doubt they're connected in any way, but it appears the press is already jumping to that conclusion," Ryan said. "Just watch this."

Beth sat on the sofa, her eyes fixed on the screen.

"I see what you mean," she said. "I guess it's more sensational if they link the cases, but there's absolutely no evidence to support it."

"And let's hope they don't find any," Ryan replied. "The body of the woman must have been in horrid condition if they couldn't identify her."

"We can't wait for Phillips and Williams to figure this out," Beth said.

"I agree. If we assume Sarah was attacked at Jefferson Peak, someone must've known she was going to be there."

"Or they followed her there."

"I guess it's possible someone could've been hiding at the peak, waiting for a random stranger to come along, but I think that's low odds," Ryan said.

"So, you're saying it's someone who's met or knows Sarah?"

"Yeah. That's what I think," Ryan replied.

"That's a lot of people to sort through," Beth said.

"True, but we have to start somewhere."

- 5.1 -

FRANK WILLIS PULLED his rusted red pickup to the side of the gravel road a mile from the Jefferson Park ranger station. Jasper and Jake, his Kentucky Coonhounds, bellowed in anticipation from the bed of the truck.

It was at that point where the dogs picked up a strong scent yesterday afternoon before darkness brought an end to their search. Sgt. Williams and Patrolman Mitch Donnelly agreed to meet Willis the next morning to pick up where they left off. The officers were waiting when Willis pulled up.

"It's really unusual for coyotes to drag a meal this fer. Some other critter must've wanted it," Willis said, loading up his cheek with a pinch of snuff. "But I'm pretty sure my boys was gettin' close ta somethin' yesterday."

"We're talking about a woman's body, Frank. Not a meal," Donnelly said, cringing. "Can you watch the language?"

"Sorry. This is a fust for me an' da boys," he replied.

"Well, I hope you're right about being close. Without finding more of the woman's corpse, it's gonna be damned hard to figure out what happened to her," Williams said. "Let's get going."

Willis unleashed the dogs and they leapt from the truck bed. They scurried, noses to the ground, out to a clearing that led to a border of tall pines.

A few minutes later Jake, the larger of the hounds, became excited, lifting his nose to the air and howling every few strides.

FALLEN from SIGHT

The second dog soon joined in. The scent took them across the opening and into the dense tree line.

"They's close ta somethin'," Willis said, jogging to catch up.

Frank Willis was a wiry backwoods hunter, and it wasn't his first time chasing coonhounds. He and the much younger patrolman were able to stay within sight of the rust-red hounds, but the barrel-chested sergeant was falling further behind, stopping frequently, hands on his knees, sucking in air.

The men raised their arms to protect their faces from tree limbs as the dogs galloped forward through the forest. The trees began to thin before opening up to a fast-running stream. The dogs continued down the streambed before stopping one hundred yards away, where they began howling and circling.

Willis and the patrolman had almost reached the hounds before Williams emerged from the woods. He stopped, leaning against a tree, unable to maintain the pace.

Williams looked up to see Willis in the distance leashing his dogs and pulling them back from the edge of the stream.

"Sergeant! Get down here!" the patrolman called back.

Williams dug deep for what little strength he had remaining and jogged down the bank of the stream with the agility of a three-legged buffalo.

The stench of decay greeted him before he arrived. The smell of death watered his eyes and burned his nostrils. He stopped, pulling a handkerchief from his pocket to cover his face.

The upper torso of a woman lay at the side of the stream. Her clothes had been stripped from her eviscerated body. The face was sunken and decayed beyond recognition, her hair was red and matted, and her arms were ravaged to the bone.

"I doubt this was a canoeing accident," Donnelly said, stepping away.

Willis' dogs continued to howl as they strained at the ends of their leashes.

"You can take your hounds back now, Frank. They've done their job," Williams said. "Donnelly, stay here and make sure the coyotes don't do any more damage. I'm gonna call the coroner and meet him out by the road."

- 5.2 -

IT WAS APPROACHING NOON when James Rigby's phone rang in his office. He winced when he saw the caller ID.

"Have you been watching the news this morning?" Fred Warren blurted.

"Yes, Fred. It would be pretty hard to ignore, wouldn't it?"

"The cops say they've got reason to suspect foul play. Are you sure you're not involved in that Campbell girl's disappearance? You didn't do something stupid, did you?"

"I told you I had nothin' to do with it, nor do I have any idea who did," Rigby replied.

"Every cop in the state is gonna come snooping around. They'll find out what she knew, and then they'll come after us."

"There's no need for you to get all nervous. I found the file in her desk with the initial test results. There are no other copies."

"What if she kept a second copy at home? Or maybe she took notes."

"She had no reason to do that. I convinced her the first tests were faulty."

"Then why did she keep a copy of those results? She must've been suspicious of something."

"Listen! This whole damned mess is your fault!" Rigby shouted. "If you'd done what I'd told you, Sarah Campbell would've never been able to get a copy. We're lucky no one else was curious enough to access the report before we destroyed it."

D.R. Shoultz

"If anyone finds out about the altered data, I'm not going down alone!" Warren threatened.

"No one's gonna find out. Like you said, it will take decades for any sign of pollution to show up in the water supply. Just stay calm and we're in the clear."

"I sure hope you're right," Warren replied.

"All you need to do is relax and figure out how you're gonna enjoy that wad of cash I gave you."

Rigby slammed down the phone and stood to retrieve his sport coat from the corner rack. He slipped it on and strode past his assistant seated in the outer lobby.

"I'll be back in ten minutes," he called over his shoulder.

He quickly traversed the parking lot, staring past workers he encountered along the way. Sue Evans was at her desk when Rigby arrived at the sales office.

"Two visits in one week. This is a first," she said, looking up at her boss.

"I was watching the news this morning, and just wondered if you've heard any more than what's been on TV."

"No, but what's been reported scares the hell out of me," Sue replied. "Who would want to hurt Sarah? I sure hope that girl's body isn't connected to her disappearance."

"I can't believe what's happening. I liked it better when car break-ins were the big news around here," Rigby said.

"Yeah. Me, too."

"We didn't get a chance to talk after the Nelson boy and Sarah's sister left yesterday. What did they discuss with you?"

"Their questions were similar to Detective Phillips. They wanted to know if Sarah had any disputes with her coworkers, and I told them any disagreements were strictly business related and not personal."

"They want to know anything else?"

"Yeah. They did ask something Phillips didn't."

"What was that?"

"They wanted to know if anyone was acting differently since Sarah had gone missing, if anyone was nervous or acting peculiar."

"What did you say?"

"I just said everyone was concerned and worried."

"Even more worried now," Rigby added. "They must be frightened to death after the recent news."

- 5.3 -

THE SBI REGIONAL OFFICE assigned Detective Ozzie Baker to work with Chief Adkins' team on the Sarah Campbell and Jane Doe cases. Parsons Creek PD was directed to conduct joint meetings with Baker. A bachelor, Baker arranged for extended stay lodging in Boone during what could be a long assignment.

Adkins, Detective Phillips, Sgt. Williams, and Officer Donnelly joined Baker for their first meeting in the chief's conference room.

Baker, with his distinguished-looking grey hair, dark tailored jacket, and neatly knotted tie, was a stark contrast to Detective Phillips in his wrinkled dress shirt and open collar.

"I've just received the test results from the state lab," Phillips began. "They determined the blood evidence on the stick matches Sarah Campbell's DNA samples, confirming she'd been assaulted."

"Any prints on the weapon?" Adkins asked.

"No. The surface was too rough."

"One of the sets of prints on the backpack hadn't been matched. Any luck there?" Williams asked.

"No, they're still searching state and federal databases for a match."

"What about the Jane Doe case?" Detective Baker asked. "What has the coroner determined, if anything?"

"Only that the torso found at the stream does match the body parts found nearly a mile away at the ranger station," Phillips said. "He estimates the remains were in the water for several days before they were discovered. He's still trying to determine the time and cause of death."

"Can he provide anything more specific about the victim to enable a search of missing persons?" Baker asked.

"The body is female, red shoulder-length hair, and probably in her teens to early twenties," Phillips replied.

"How much of what we've uncovered do you think we should release?" Adkins asked.

"We've already announced foul play in Sarah Campbell's disappearance, but I don't think we should confirm we've identified a stick that was used as a weapon," Phillips replied.

"I agree," Baker interrupted. "And I think we should continue to be clear there's nothing linking the Jane Doe death to Sarah Campbell's disappearance."

Phillips turned toward his chief and rolled his eyes.

"So, am I safe in assuming your interviews and investigations haven't identified any suspects?" Baker asked.

"You would be correct," Phillips replied, mocking Baker's tone.

"We have persons of interest," Sgt. Williams added, "but it's too early to classify any of them as suspects."

"I need to understand what's leading you to these conclusions. I'd like to spend some time with you getting up to speed," Baker said, turning to Phillips.

Phillips grimaced. "You're welcome to read our reports and make suggestions, but I'm not going to relive the past week with you."

"Then I guess I'll just have to take time during these status meetings with everyone present to ask questions," Baker replied. "I don't know how else I can effectively deploy state resources."

Phillips turned to Chief Adkins with a what's-with-this-guy look.

"Phillips, why don't you and Williams take a long coffee break with Detective Baker and provide what he needs? We'll see how we can simplify this process as we move forward."

"Sure," Phillips grumbled. "But could I have a quick word in your office first?"

"Fine. I think we're done here," Adkins replied. "I'll see everyone at the next update."

Phillips was the first to exit the conference room, hurrying ahead of Adkins to the chief's office.

"Chief, I've already got my hands full with these two cases, and now you're asking me to spoon-feed this Sean Connery look-alike," Phillips ranted as he stood before Adkins' desk. "I thought he was here to coordinate state resources behind the scenes, not to interfere with my investigations."

"These cases are in our jurisdiction, and as long as we cooperate with the state, we have the lead," Adkins replied. "Surely, you can spend enough time with Baker to keep him up to date."

"He doesn't strike me as someone who follows orders, and I've already got Nelson and the Campbell twin conducting their own investigation."

"Don't worry about Ryan Nelson and Beth Campbell. They're obviously concerned and have a right to search for Sarah," Adkins said. "Go spend a few minutes with Baker. It'll keep the SBI off our backs, and besides, he could end up being a valuable asset."

FALLEN from SIGHT

- 5.4 -

SOMETHING RYAN NELSON asked kept rolling around in Sue Evans' head.

Have you noticed anyone acting strangely since Sarah went missing?

She could only think of one person.

Sue grabbed the key to Sarah's desk and stepped out of her office. She sat in Sarah's desk chair and unlocked the drawers.

One by one she opened each drawer and ran her finger up and down the labels on the folders. There was no customer file for John Brewer.

Sue returned to her office, found Ryan's business card and dialed his number.

Beth and Ryan had just left the Jefferson Park ranger station where they'd talked with rangers about the body they'd discovered. They were on their way to Sarah's home for Beth to retrieve the rest of her things. Ryan's cellphone rang as they stepped into the house.

"This is Ryan."

"It's Sue Evans. I was wondering if you could do me a favor."

"Yeah. Sure. What is it?"

"Is Sarah's leather purse at her house? It's the large one that doubles as her briefcase."

"I think so. It's in her bedroom on the dresser."

"Could you see if there's a spiral notebook inside? It would be about five by seven inches or so."

"Give me a minute."

Ryan hurried back to Sarah's bedroom and opened her purse. He pushed items to the side in search of the notebook, but didn't find it.

"I don't see a notebook. It could have been one of the items taken by the forensic team. They really gave this place a once-over."

"That's okay. It's probably nothing important."

"What're you looking for?" Ryan asked.

"I thought she might have taken notes during a customer visit last Friday. Jim Rigby was looking for the information."

"Did you check her desk?"

"Yeah. I just checked it a second time. Jim searched her desk earlier, but didn't find a file on the customer. I thought Sarah might have what he was looking for in her notebook."

"Were you with Rigby when he searched Sarah's desk?"

"Yeah, except for a brief moment when I stepped away for a phone call," she replied. "Why do you ask?"

"Just curious," Ryan said. "You might call the police department and see if they have the notebook."

"It's probably nothing worth bothering them about," Sue replied. "Thanks for checking."

Ryan pushed his phone back into his pocket and stood, staring across Sarah's bedroom.

"Who was that?" Beth asked.

"Sue Evans. She was looking for information from a notebook. She thought it might be in Sarah's purse, but the notebook's not there."

"You look puzzled. What is it?"

"I'm not sure, but it appears Sue Evans suspects something."

FALLEN from SIGHT

- 5.5 -

JAMES RIGBY GUIDED HIS black Escalade up the winding entrance to his sprawling ranch home perched on the side of Raven Ridge Mountain. The sun had just hidden behind the layered mountains thirty miles away.

The estate-sized home was his refuge. It was a fifteen-minute drive from the Rolling Ridge development and a safe distance from work-related interruptions.

His grey striped Maine Coon cat, Reggie, greeted him at the door to the garage, brushing against one leg and then the other. Rigby reached down to stroke the animal's head. The enormous feline provided companionship when Rigby needed it, but the cat was sufficiently independent to not require much attention.

Rigby took the lid off a treat jar on the kitchen counter and plucked a morsel from inside. He tossed the treat toward the family room and the cat sped away. As the portly feline returned for more, Rigby's cellphone rang in his coat pocket.

The ID read *Unknown Caller.*

He started to return the phone to his pocket, but decided to answer.

"Yeah. What is it?"

"Don't hang up, and don't call the cops. It would be a big mistake."

The muffled voice was hard to understand. It sounded like a man, but not anyone he recognized.

"You need to gather one million in unmarked bills, and I'll…"

"You must have the wrong number," Rigby interrupted.

"I'm speaking to James Rigby, and I can bring you and your flashy development crashing down if you don't cooperate."

"What are you talking about?"

"The county inspector and you are a little too chummy, don't you think?"

"Who is this? Who've you been talking to?" Rigby asked, his expansive forehead beginning to glisten.

"I have a reliable source. Do what I say, and you'll stay a free man."

Reliable source?

"Get the one million gathered by this time tomorrow, and I'll call with further instructions."

"You don't know what you're talking about. You can forget about getting any money."

"You're in no position to negotiate, Rigby! Bribing county officials is one thing, but killing an innocent girl to cover it up is quite another."

"You're crazy! I haven't killed anyone!"

"Yeah. I'm crazy as a fox. Just get the money, fat boy."

The line went silent. Rigby hurried to the front of the house and peered out the wide picture window, wondering if anyone had followed him home.

Dusk had fallen. There were no lights or movement, only a dark tree-lined tunnel leading to the main road.

He took out his cellphone and began to dial Fred Warren, but pulled his finger back from the *CALL* key.

Warren couldn't handle the pressure. He'd go to the cops.

FALLEN from SIGHT

Rigby had liquidated all his disposal assets to pay off Warren. It would take days, maybe longer, to come up with a million dollars.

He went to his liquor cabinet and poured a double shot of bourbon. His feline companion jumped atop the counter as Rigby lifted the glass and tossed back the drink.

Frozen in thought, he reached to stroke the head of the large cat.

"What do I do now, old boy?"

- Day 6 -

PATCHES LEAPT TO THE CENTER of Ryan's bed, signaling the sun had risen. It had become a morning routine. The dog nudged Ryan's side with his nose and waited for his new master to stir.

"Alright! Alright! I'm getting up," Ryan grumbled.

Beth was already at the kitchen table when Ryan came down the hall with the high-spirited spaniel prancing at his heels.

"You're up early," Ryan said.

She looked up, eyes red and pooling.

"I couldn't sleep. Sarah's been gone a week. Where could she be that's safe?"

Ryan stepped to Beth's side and placed his hand on her shoulder.

"She's out there, and I know that we'll find her."

"Have you seen the news?" she asked.

Ryan shook his head.

"The girl found in Jefferson Park was murdered. The coroner said she'd been bound and strangled."

"I'm sure there's no connection to Sarah," he replied, unable to keep the doubt from his voice.

"Do you think we could head back to Rolling Ridge this morning?" Beth asked.

"Are you concerned that we've missed something?"

"I don't think we can rely on what Sue Evans and James Rigby have told us. We need to talk to more people."

Ryan sat across from Beth, noticing a pad of paper in front of her.

"What's that?" he asked.

"These are the names I've heard mentioned since we began our search," she replied. "Surely, one of them knows something."

"Why is Guy Fletcher's name scratched off?" he asked, craning his neck to read the list.

"I called him after you went to bed. He still claims his band was performing in Charleston the weekend Sarah went missing. This time he gave me the names of three people who could confirm it."

"And?"

"And his story checks out. He's a flake, but it doesn't look like he had anything to do with Sarah's disappearance."

"Who do you want to see at Rolling Ridge?"

"Lance Baldwin gets back today. I think we should start with him," Beth said. "He's the only other sales associate in the office, and he probably works with the same people as Sarah."

"I've met Lance a few times," Ryan said. "He's about our age and seemed a little intense. Sarah tells me he likes the finer things—clothes, watches, cars. He even worked nights at a fancy restaurant in Boone parking cars for extra cash."

"I'd also like to talk with Rigby's foreman. He has to know the subcontractors better than anyone."

"I've worked with Jeb. He's like a trained coonhound," Ryan replied. "I get the impression he's pretty good at following Rigby's commands, but that's about it."

Beth stood and walked to the counter for a cup of coffee. She turned with a cup in her hand and leaned back against the cabinets.

"My boss called and asked when to expect me back," she said. "I'm not sure I could go back to work given the way things stand now."

"Same with me," Ryan replied. "My hands are healing, but there's no way I could concentrate on work."

"Maybe we'll get some good news this weekend."

FALLEN from SIGHT

- 6.1 -

JAMES RIGBY'S EYES CRACKED open as he pried his head from the arm of the sofa. The bourbon had rendered him unconscious around 3:00 a.m. He squinted at the wall clock in the hall, but couldn't tell if the hands were at 6:00 or 12:30.

As his mind sought solid footing, the haunting voice from last night's call rose inside his head.

A reliable source…

One million cash…

I'll call tomorrow…

Rigby pushed himself up and slid his feet to the floor. He sat for a moment, rubbing his eyes, before rocking to stand on unsteady legs. His ever-present cat ran to his side. Rigby nudged it back with his knee. It hissed and ran off.

After creeping his way to the kitchen, Rigby reached into the refrigerator for a bottle of water. Leaning on the open door, he drank half the contents before lowering it from his lips.

He found his cellphone on the kitchen counter and checked the time. It was 6:30. He stared at the display for several seconds, wondering what to do next. He jammed the phone into his pocket.

The real estate developer's head was pounding like a kettle drum as he turned to see his reflection in the microwave door. His thinning hair was pointed in all directions, looking like he'd been struck by lightning. He reached up and slicked it back to this head.

Rigby took another drink of water and stood staring across the room.

A reliable source?

RIGBY ARRIVED AT WORK later than usual to find Ryan Nelson's Ford Bronco parked in one of the visitor spaces directly in front of the sales office. Not fully recovered from his hangover, he coasted into his reserved space and trudged to his office, closing the door behind him.

Saturday was typically the busiest day of the week for the Rolling Ridge sales staff, but with the exception of Rigby, the management office was empty. Sitting behind his desk, he picked up the phone and dialed.

"Do you think it's wise to call me at home?" Fred Warren answered in a hushed tone.

"Have you been talking to anyone about our arrangement?" Rigby blurted.

"Of course not."

"Are you sure? Not even your wife?"

"No one," Warren replied. "What's up?"

"Someone knows," Rigby said.

"Who? How do you know?"

"I can't say more, but you need to be straight with me," Rigby said firmly. "If there's any chance you let it slip, tell me."

"There's no chance," Warren replied. "Everyone on my end is convinced Rolling Ridge is in the clear. What about your foreman? Could he have found out?"

"Jeb only knows what I tell him," Rigby shot back, "and I haven't told him a damned thing!"

"There's not much more I can do unless you tell me who's spooking you," Warren said.

"Never mind," Rigby said. "I'll handle it."

Rigby disconnected and stepped from his office to the front window, staring across the parking lot at Ryan Nelson's Bronco.

"This can't be good," he muttered.

LANCE BALDWIN FINISHED a phone call as Beth and Ryan waited in the sales office lobby. Dressed in a casual shirt and slacks, he rose and introduced himself, offering Beth a faint hug. He then extended his hand to Ryan. Standing eye level to him, his handshake was firm.

"I can't believe what's happened," Lance said. "I hated being away. I wanted to rush back, but Sue assured me there was nothing I could do."

"Yeah. It's been tough," Beth said. "But we're still hoping for the best."

"Do you have a few minutes to talk?" Ryan asked.

"Sure, but Sue's out today, so I might need to step away if her phone rings," he replied, leading them to a sitting area across the lobby.

"We've been wracking our brains for days. Can you think of anyone who'd want to harm Sarah?" Beth began.

"Absolutely not. When I first heard she'd disappeared, I hoped she'd been called away unexpectedly, but with these recent announcements, I'm just praying she's not seriously hurt."

"Had you noticed Sarah acting differently prior to her disappearance, or anyone acting strangely towards her?" Ryan asked.

Lance thought.

"She had seemed more reserved, keeping to herself," Lance replied. "But I assumed she was just focused on business. We'd been busy following the announcement of phase two."

"What about her relationships with other employees? Anything unusual?" Beth asked.

Again, Lance paused.

"This is probably nothing, but about two weeks ago, and out of the blue, she asked if I trusted Jeb Jones."

"Trust him about what?" Ryan asked, leaning forward.

"That's what I asked her, but she wouldn't say. I told her I had no reason not to trust him."

"Did the subject ever come up again?" Ryan asked.

"Nope. That was it."

"Do you know if Jeb's around today?" Beth asked.

"I doubt it," he replied. "If he is, he'd be out at one of the construction sites. Not much happens at the management office on weekends."

Beth turned to Ryan with a frown, frustrated their meeting with Jones would have to wait.

"What's the dynamic between James Rigby and the sales team?" Ryan asked.

"We get along fine," Lance replied. "He's been happy with our sales."

"I'd heard from Sue that Rigby asked to unlock Sarah's desk, looking for a customer file. Does that sound like something normal?"

"Not really, but Sue tells me nothing's been normal since Sarah disappeared."

"Would Sarah keep anything in her desk that she wouldn't want Rigby to see?" Ryan asked.

"I wouldn't think so. Our real estate files are kept audit-ready, so Rigby, our clients, or even the Real Estate Commission could see them at any time. Why do you ask?"

"I just find it unusual that Rigby would search through Sarah's desk for something so trivial, something that could easily be recreated by just asking the customer."

"Are you suggesting he was looking for something else?" Lance asked.

"I'm not sure," Ryan said, "but it makes me wonder."

Sue Evans' line rang.

"I should take this," Lance said, standing.

"That's okay," Ryan replied. "We're finished. Let us know if you think of anything else."

RIGBY STEPPED BACK from the window and watched as Ryan and Beth left the sales office. He waited until they pulled out of the parking lot before moving to the front porch.

Before he could walk down the steps, a sedan entered the lot and pulled to the front of the real estate building. A middle-aged man and woman stepped from their car. The prospective buyers sent Rigby back into his office. He'd have to wait to find out what Ryan and Beth wanted.

Rigby sat behind his desk and pulled open the center drawer. Rummaging through the contents, he found a stack of business cards bound by a rubber band. He flipped through the stack and pulled one from the middle. Setting it beside the phone, he dialed.

"Camp Creek Mortgage. This is Jarod."

"This is James Rigby. Is Max in today?"

"Just a minute."

"Hello, Mr. Rigby. How can I help?"

"I'm looking to gather some cash to invest in my business," Rigby replied. "How long would it take to get an equity loan against my home?"

"Get the paperwork to me today, and depending on the amount, I could possibly push it through by the end of next week."

"Next week?" Rigby exclaimed. "I thought I was a better customer than that."

"What size loan are you looking to arrange?" Max asked.

"I need a million as soon as possible, or this opportunity will set sail without me."

"Sorry, but I can't see approving that size loan in less time."

"Then I'll take my business elsewhere!" Rigby shouted, slamming down the phone.

The troubled real estate developer sat thinking for a long moment, tapping his fingers on his desk in a snare drumbeat. Finally, he reached for the Camp Creek Mortgage business card and flipped it over. Handwritten on the back was:

Jack Spathe - 708-919-8899 – Personal Loans

- 6.2 -

CHIEF ADKINS' TEAM GATHERED for the morning status meeting in the conference room next to his office. Empty coffee cups, notepads, and newspapers were scattered before the seven lawmen seated at the oval table. Detective Phillips was the last to enter. He exchanged glances with Detective Baker at the far end of the table and then took a seat near the door.

"Let's review the Jane Doe case first," Adkins began. "What do we have, Phillips?"

"It's a homicide case now," Phillips replied, flipping open his spiral notebook. "The coroner confirmed lacerations to her neck and wrists were consistent with being bound. The victim is a young girl in her late teens to early twenties. Time of death is still not determined, but it was likely a week or more prior to discovering the body."

"What about DNA evidence? Any matches to missing persons?" Adkins asked.

"Too early. Tissue samples have been sent to the state lab," Phillips replied. "We've started sorting through databases, matching what little information we have—red hair, blue eyes, slight build, approximately five-four, Caucasian."

"And?"

"There've been more than fifty missing person cases matching this Jane Doe in the past year alone, and that's just from a two-hundred-mile radius," Phillips said. "They're mostly runaways, many from foster homes or dysfunctional families, some with criminal records."

"I recommend that the SBI take over this case," Baker announced from the end of the table with his baritone voice. "You guys have your hands full with the Campbell matter, and the SBI has much more homicide experience."

"These cases are within our jurisdiction," Phillips argued, "and should be managed together to understand any connections or overlaps."

"There's no evidence linking the two cases," Baker said matter-of-factly, focusing his comment toward Adkins.

"They're both assaults on young women, and evidence in both crimes was found in Jefferson Park. It's way too early to rule out a connection," Phillips argued, leaning his boney forearms on the table.

"I have no problem with you helping my team process the evidence and sharing your experience," Adkins interrupted, "but we can only have one lead, and that's Phillips."

Detective Phillips leaned back and turned toward Baker with a take-that expression.

"And Phillips," Adkins continued. "Find a way to get Detective Baker involved in the Jane Doe investigation. It makes no sense having a man with his experience just running reports back and forth to Charlotte."

Phillips and Baker stared at each other in a country mouse-city mouse standoff, Phillips in his wrinkled, off-the-rack, blue sport coat and Baker in his charcoal Brooks Brothers blazer.

"What's next on the Campbell case?" Adkins asked.

"Still no match on the fourth set of prints from the backpack," Phillips replied. "If we don't get a hit from federal databases, we may have to collect samples from her friends and colleagues."

"They don't have to cooperate without a warrant," Baker said.

"I understand, but we can at least rule out those who volunteer."

"What else?" Adkins asked.

"We're pulling Campbell's phone records from her office phone and cellphone in an attempt to trace her activities in the days leading to her disappearance," Phillips said.

"Have you arranged for the court orders?" Baker asked.

"They're all set," Phillips replied.

"Okay. Let's get moving," Adkins said, standing.

The room quickly emptied, with Baker rising slowly as Phillips continued to review his meeting notes. Neither wanted to initiate the peace treaty ordered by Adkins.

Baker stepped slowly toward the Parsons Creek detective at the front of the room.

"I'll run with the Jane Doe tissue samples and try to narrow down the missing persons matching her description," Baker offered.

"Sounds good," Phillips replied, looking up from his notes. "And if there are people you think we should be questioning, let me know."

"Yeah. I'll do that."

- 6.3 -

"WAKE UP, MISSY. You've made bail."

Brown County Corrections was printed in bold letters across the breast pocket of the jailer's short sleeved white shirt. An ample gut protruded over a belt struggling to hold up dark slacks which gathered at his ankles.

The slight, dark-haired woman passed out on the prison cot wore purple satin shorts and a white tank top. Her leopard print canvas shoes lay on the floor beside her.

She pulled back her long, tangled hair with one hand to reveal a youthful face smeared with makeup. She stared up through glazed eyes at the man leaning over her.

"Leave me the fuck alone," she snarled before her head fell back to the cot.

"Missy! You're free to go! Bail's been posted!" he called louder.

Two women whose youth was in their rearview mirror sat on cots in the cell across the aisle. Dressed in spandex leggings and clingy silk blouses, one had purple hair and the other's was a brassy blonde. Their sleep deprived eyes were transfixed on the jailer.

"Her name's Jewell," the brassy-haired woman offered.

"Yeah. I'm sure it is," the jailer replied with a smirk.

He lightly tapped the young woman on her face with the back of his hand.

Her eyes cracked open again, and she tilted her head to look up.

"Let me sleep, you fat bastard!   Get outta here!" she growled.

"Suit yourself," he said, "but Prince Charming may not come back tomorrow."

"I'll take my chances," she said, her head falling back onto the drool-stained mattress.

"Does the prince have enough bail money for two hardworking girls?" the brassy-haired woman asked, standing to get a better look through the bars.

"Sit tight, Cinderella," the guard replied. "He specifically asked for this one."

The portly jailer moved to the cell door.

"I'm done in here," he called out.

His associate seated at the end of the hallway hit the release button for cell number five and the door slid to the side. After the jailer stepped through, the steel door slammed shut with an eerie metal clank.

He then proceeded down the short aisle between the rows of cells where he stepped through a door into the outer chambers.

A tall, clean-shaven, young man with thick dark hair dressed in jeans and a blue sport coat sat waiting at a table. Seeing the jailer, he tossed his cigarette to the floor and stomped it out.

"I've told you before! No smoking inside the jailhouse," the jailer shouted.

"Yeah. Yeah. Where's the girl?" the young man asked, standing.

"She's sleeping off whatever she's been taking," the guard replied.

"She's not coming?"

"Not today. She refuses to leave."

"I've already paid her bail. Here are the court orders," he said, sticking documents in the jailer's face.

"If she doesn't want to leave, she doesn't have to go," the jailer said, stepping away. "She'll be here when you come back."

The young man dropped his arms to his side and glared at the guard as he disappeared back through the door. He waited a couple of minutes before walking out the front of the Brown County Corrections Center toward a waiting truck in the parking lot.

A stocky man with salt-and-pepper hair and weekend stubble sat in the driver's seat of the new pickup. The setting sun had given way to amber streetlight which bounced off the vehicle's high-gloss finish.

With agitation on his face, the man gripped the steering wheel with muscled forearms as he watched his partner climb into the passenger seat.

"What's up, Slim? Where's Jewell?"

"Don't call me that!" his partner grumbled. "I got enough of that in high school."

"Around me, you're Slim. Get over it. Now where is she?"

"The screw said she's hung over and doesn't want to leave."

"Doesn't want to leave? It's Saturday!" the driver screamed. "I've got clients waiting in Charlotte!"

"Maybe it's time to cut this one loose," Slim replied. "She keeps running back to Tennessee and getting strung out."

"Yeah, but her daddy calls me as soon as she shows up, and she's proven to be a gold mine."

"So, what do you want me to do, J.D.?" Slim asked.

"Heather could've filled in if you hadn't sold her off to those drunken hunters," the beady-eyed J.D. scowled.

"You weren't around, and I figured you wouldn't turn down five bills for a couple hours of her time. How'd I know they'd get carried away?"

"You've left us with few options," the older partner complained. "Everyone else is taken this weekend."

"A couple other girls are in there," Slim said, tipping his head toward the jail. "I overheard a deputy say that he found them turning tricks behind Big Jim's Playhouse."

"I don't have time to break in new girls. Besides, my clients like 'em young. Now get back in there and spring Jewell. Slip the jailer a fifty if you have to."

- 6.4 -

RIGBY RETURNED TO THE PRIVACY of his home to place a call to Jack Spathe. It had been two years since he'd spoken to the New Jersey loan shark.

At that time, Charlotte banks refused to loan money to Rigby for the phase two land purchase since he still owed creditors on the phase one development. Rigby acquired a loan from Spathe to pay off phase one creditors. The off-the-books transaction was never seen by the Charlotte banks, and his loan application for the phase two purchase was approved.

"A MIL IN CASH?" Spathe shouted. "What kinda trouble are ya in this time?"

"You'll get your money back," Rigby promised. "That's all you need to know."

"Plus twenty percent," Spathe shot back. "And ya got ninety days."

"Yeah. Yeah. I'm familiar with your terms. Can you have it ready by tomorrow?"

"Tomorrow? Who da ya tink I am? Wells Fargo?"

"Then when?"

"Wednesday next week. Maybe Tuesday if everything goes good," Spathe replied.

Rigby sat thinking, his eyes nervously darting around the room.

"If that's the best you can do," Rigby conceded, "but if you can arrange it sooner, let me know."

"I'll call ya as soon as I have it and letcha know where ta meet me ta pick it up," Spathe said. "Good doin' bidness witch ya."

Rigby slammed his phone onto the coffee table and headed to his living room bar. His cat circled around and then between Rigby's legs, seeking attention. Rigby failed to notice.

He looked down at his watch before pouring a double bourbon. It had been nearly twenty-four hours since the blackmailer's call.

He tossed back the drink and poured another before going back to sit on the sofa. He stared at his phone on the coffee table, waiting for it to ring.

Only Fred Warren knows of the payoff, Rigby thought. *But Campbell knows about the soil tests.*

Another hour passed, and the room grew darker as the sun set below the pines. Rigby was on his fourth drink, pacing the room with the glass in his hand.

Reggie sensed his owner's anxiety and called out from the sofa with screeching meows.

"Shut the hell up!" Rigby shouted.

The cat ran to the far end of the sofa and resumed its nervous calls. Rigby grabbed the bulky feline, took him to the spare bedroom, and tossed him inside. He walked back down the hall as Reggie scratched at the door.

Rigby finished off what remained in his glass and walked to the bar. As he began to pour another shot of bourbon, he looked down to his shaking hand. He set the bottle back on the counter and stuffed the cork in the top just as his phone rang.

Rigby whipped his head around and stared at the phone for two rings before reaching to pick it up.

"I trust you have good news," the muffled voice began.

Rigby's blood pressure spiked.

"I can get the money by Wednesday, maybe Tuesday, but no sooner," he replied. "I can't just walk into a bank and get one million in cash. It takes time."

The line was silent.

"Did you hear me?" Rigby asked louder.

"Yeah. I heard. I'll give you 'til Monday, but no later."

"That's impossible! I just got off the phone with my lender. It can't be sooner than Tuesday."

"Get it Monday, or you'll rot in prison for murder," the blackmailer replied.

"Murder? I didn't murder anyone."

"Tell that to the cops on Monday if I don't get my money. If you think I'm bluffing, go see what's in the back of your Escalade."

"My Escalade? What are you talking about?"

"Get me the money on Monday!"

The phone went silent.

Rigby raced to the garage. He went to the back of his black SUV and hit the tailgate button. The door slowly rose as he bent down to see what was inside.

A ball of green clothing was stuffed against the back seat. His heart pumped as he grabbed the garment and spread it out on the floor of the SUV.

It was a woman's sweater. Dried bloodstains were splattered on the neck and shoulder.

"Shit!"

- 6.5 -

"WHAT TOOK YOU SO LONG? It's after midnight."

The sour-faced man greeting J.D. at the door of the roadside hotel was dressed in slacks and an open-collar shirt. Fast food wrappers were strewn across the coffee table behind him, and he held an uncorked bottle of scotch in his left hand.

"It'll be worth the wait," J.D. replied.

He stepped to the side, revealing the dark-haired teen standing behind him. Jewell was still glassy-eyed from the four-hour drive. Cars and semi-trailers whisked past over her shoulder, buzzing up and down I-77.

"She looks like hell," the john replied. "Where did you find this one?"

"Her name's Jewell. She just needs a little time to freshen up. Don't you, Hon?" J.D. asked.

"Yeah. Sure," the teen mumbled.

The middle-aged man took a step forward and studied the girl in the tank top and satin shorts.

"A shower might be a good change of pace," he said, reaching to brush Jewell's cheek. She jerked her head back.

"Usual charge up front," J.D. said, holding his hand palm up. "Hurt her, and I'll find you."

"Yeah. Yeah. I got your money," he replied, reaching to his back pocket for his wallet. "I'll be finished in a couple of hours. You can pick her up any time after that."

"I'll be waiting," J.D. said. "And no kinky stuff. She has other appointments tonight."

D.R. Shoultz

"Come on, Sweetie. It's gettin' late," the man said, grasping Jewell's hand and pulling her inside.

As the door closed, she looked back at J.D., hopelessness etched on her young face.

- Day 7 -

WITH THE JANE DOE MURDER unsolved and Sarah Campbell still missing, there were no days off for the Parsons Creek police. The small-town police department had been on twelve-hour shifts for four days, and Chief Adkins maintained twice daily status meetings with his senior staff. Nerves were on edge and tempers were short.

Detective Phillips waited for the grumbling lawmen gathered in Chief Adkins' conference room to look up from their coffee and Sunday sports pages. He briefly made eye contact with Detective Baker, who'd moved forward from his customary seat at the end of the table, now seated nearly across from Phillips.

"Okay. Let's get started," Phillips called out. "We were able to get fingerprint samples from several of Sarah Campbell's friends, associates, and others she came in contact with on a regular basis. So far, there are no matches to the fingerprints on the backpack."

"Anyone refuse to be printed?" Chief Adkins asked.

"Not yet, but we've just begun. Many of Ms. Campbell's associates weren't at work yesterday."

"Any leads surface while gathering the prints?" Detective Baker asked.

"No, not really. Most asked what we knew or if we thought she'd still be found safe," Phillips replied.

"What about the Jane Doe case?" Adkins asked, turning to Baker.

"I've been able to narrow the number of missing women who match our victim," Baker replied. "Of the several hundred over the past year, I'm down to eighteen and still waiting on DNA to narrow it further."

"Any of the eighteen stick out as probable matches to our Jane Doe?" Adkins asked.

"Hard to tell at this point," Baker replied. "There are seven teenage runaways with drug addictions on the list. The toxicology report from the coroner indicates our victim was a meth user, so it's possible one of these seven may end up being a match."

"Have you checked to see if any of them have recent arrest records?" Phillips asked.

"Yeah. I checked, but there were no hits. Even if any of them had been picked up recently, it's likely we wouldn't know. They take on false identities. The lives of these young women spiral downward quickly. And their stories don't usually end well."

"How so?" Adkins asked.

"They'll do anything for their next fix and a warm place to sleep. Many end up victims of sex traffickers. The ringleaders give them new names, new identities, and a life they can't escape."

"You sound like you know something about this," Phillips said.

"I worked Charlotte Homicide for twenty years, and I've come across more than a few of these cases. The demand for young girls and boys in big cities is staggering—and sickening."

Silent stares were directed at Baker from those around the table.

"It's not something we've experienced in these parts," Sgt. Williams said with a dismissive tone.

"Not that you know of," Baker replied.

"Would it be worth contacting the relatives of the seven missing women to see what they can provide?" Adkins asked.

"I can't see upsetting parents with what little we know," Baker replied. "I'd prefer to wait a day or two for the DNA to come back."

"You're probably right," Adkins said. "In the meantime, we'll continue asking the public for feedback. The calls to our hotline haven't been productive yet, but someone must know something about these cases."

"The calls coming in are mostly wackos," Williams complained. "I recommend we don't waste time on them. Our officers are already working twelve-hour shifts."

"As long as we have resources to follow up, don't disregard *any* of the calls," Adkins instructed.

Williams turned away, rolling his eyes.

"If there are no more updates, I'll see everyone back here tonight," Adkins said.

- 7.1 -

JAMES RIGBY AWOKE from a nightmare, his arms flaying. He tossed the satin sheets off his perspiring body, sending his cat fleeing the room.

With his heart pounding, Rigby sat up and turned to the clock on his nightstand. It flipped to 9:45 a.m. as his eyes and mind came back into focus. He realized the nightmare was more truth than fiction. Questions that had haunted him last evening began to circle through his mind again.

Is it really Sarah's sweater?

Should I go to the cops?

Who's doing this?

He hadn't come up with answers to any of the questions, but time was running out. The next call from his blackmailer was expected tomorrow night.

Rigby swung his feet to the floor and hurried to his closet to change. After dressing, he strode past his cat in the hall and went straight to his study. Seated behind his desk, he powered up his laptop and began entering Google searches:

Attorney-Client Privilege

Limits of Attorney-Client Privilege

Penalties for Bribery in NC

"Shit. None of this makes any sense," he muttered to himself, staring at the screen.

After an hour of reading legalese that did little to answer his questions, he reached for his phone and placed a call.

"Really, Rigby? You're calling me at home on a Sunday?"

FALLEN from SIGHT

Still in his silk pajamas, Victor Manson, Rigby's real estate attorney, had just finished a late breakfast on his 15th floor patio in Uptown Charlotte. He was deciding which football game to watch when Rigby called.

"Just shut up and listen," Rigby replied. "I need some advice, and I didn't know who else to call."

"Yeah. What have you done now?"

"Before I say anything, is this discussion protected by the attorney-client privilege?"

"That depends," Manson replied. "Are you looking for me to represent you in this matter?"

"Do you take criminal cases?"

"Of course not, but there are attorneys at my firm who do. Can you tell me what you've done?"

Rigby sat, tapping his foot on the floor.

"I haven't done anything," Rigby replied, "but someone is threatening to publicly accuse me of a crime."

"If you're innocent, what's the problem?" Manson asked.

"If he accuses me, it could open a separate can of worms that I'd just as soon avoid."

"What separate can of worms?"

"If our discussion isn't confidential, I really can't say," Rigby replied.

"Then I recommend you come into my office on Monday, and I'll get you in touch with Mike Lee, our best criminal attorney."

"Monday's too late. Could he meet today?"

"Have you been charged with any crimes?" Manson asked.

"No, I just need to talk to someone about my options."

"I'm not going to ask Mike to do a consult on a Sunday afternoon. He already works eighty hours a week. But I'm sure he'll fit you in by the end of next week."

"You're not listening! I need to see someone today!" Rigby shouted.

"Jim, if someone is threatening you, maybe you should go to the police."

"A lotta fucking help you are!" Rigby yelled, slamming down the phone.

Reggie leapt onto the desk, pleading for his overdue breakfast. Rigby swept the large feline aside with his forearm before standing and marching to the living room bar.

- 7.2 -

PATCHES LAY QUIETLY in the back seat of Ryan's Bronco, his head propped on the center armrest. On Beth's lap was a rumpled paper with a list of names and addresses. Half of the two dozen names had been scratched off. Jeb Jones was at the top of those remaining.

"So far, this has gotten us nowhere," Beth said. "All we keep hearing is what a great person Sarah *was*. Like she's already dead."

"It's better than sitting at home," Ryan replied.

"What are we looking for anyway?" she asked.

"I'm not sure, but I think we'll know when we find it."

Beth looked at Google Maps on the iPhone affixed to the dash of the Bronco.

"We're only a couple of minutes away," she said. "Are you sure it's okay to go to his home today? I thought most people around here went to church on Sunday."

"It was his idea," Ryan replied. "I suggested meeting in town, but he said he was doing some work around his house and insisted we go there this afternoon."

Beth folded the paper and stuffed it into her jeans pocket. She sat quietly for a long moment, staring down the winding, unmarked country road.

"Sarah and I often had the same dreams," she said, breaking the silence. "I had one last night. We were kids at the state fair in Raleigh, running from ride to ride with a wad of tickets in our hands. Sarah loved the Ferris wheel the most. In the dream, we were seated on the ride with a bar holding us in, circling around and around."

Beth gazed forward, eyes wide.

"The ride stopped with us at the very top. Rocking slightly, we could see for miles. I was nervous and held tight to the bar, but Sarah was never afraid. Her head pivoted from side to side, taking it all in.

"We're twins, but in many ways, she's always been my older sister—my rock. I don't know what I'll do if I lose her."

Ryan swallowed, gathering his emotions.

"I'm sure she had the same dream last night," he said.

Beth wiped her eyes and pressed her lips together, nodding.

Your destination is two hundred yards on the right, the iPhone chirped.

Patches rose up in the back seat as the SUV slowed and turned down a long gravel lane. Seeing Jeb's coonhound in the front yard, Patches barked and stuck his nose through a crack in the back window.

"Jeb told me his dog would be out," Ryan said, "and he's friendly with most people."

"I hope we're *most* people," Beth replied as Ryan pulled to a stop next to Jeb's pickup.

Dressed in jeans, a black tee shirt, and a red MAGA cap, Jeb appeared at the front door of his single-story log home. He stepped out onto the wraparound porch. Placing two fingers to his mouth, he produced a shrill whistle that brought the brown and white coonhound running to his side.

Beth and Ryan stepped from the Bronco. Patches remained in the back seat, whining and pacing.

"Hunter's friendly with dogs if you want to let yours out," Jeb called.

When Ryan opened the back door of the SUV, Patches leapt out and raced toward the playful coonhound. They circled and sniffed each other before tearing off toward an open field behind the house.

"Can I get you folks something to drink? I have a pitcher of sweet tea in the fridge," Jeb offered as Ryan and Beth stepped onto the porch.

"Thanks, but I'm fine," Beth replied as Ryan shook his head.

"Have a seat," Jeb said, pointing to the rockers on the front porch. "We can keep an eye on the dogs out here."

Beth and Ryan sat in the chairs as Jeb pulled up a rustic wooden bench made of vines and branches.

"You have a beautiful place," Beth said, her eyes scanning the tree tops. "But being from the city, I don't know if I could handle the seclusion."

"I like it this way," Jeb replied. "Hunter and I don't see many folks coming up our lane."

"Thanks for seeing us," Ryan said. "Like I said on the phone, we're trying to learn as much as we can about what Sarah was doing in the days before she disappeared."

"I've told Detective Phillips everything I could think of. He's met with most everyone at Rolling Ridge. We're all concerned."

"When did you last see Sarah?" Ryan asked.

"I saw her the Friday before she went missing. We talked briefly about a property she wanted completed for a closing. I told her I'd talk to the contractor who was holding it up."

"Who was that?" Beth asked.

"The cabinet contractor, Johnny Stratford. I got it straightened out."

"How did Sarah appear when you talked to her?" Beth asked.

"Appear?"

"Was she nervous, upset, or did she look normal?" Beth asked.

"She seemed fine. I guess she was a little upset with the delay, but nothing unusual. That's how it is around work. Sometimes things go smoothly. Sometimes they need a little push."

"And that's your job?" Ryan asked.

"Yeah. Everyone comes to me to push things along: Mr. Rigby, the sales team, everyone."

"How would you describe Sarah's relationship with the contractors and her coworkers?" Beth asked.

"I'm not sure I've thought much about it," Jeb replied as the dogs darted across the front yard. "She seemed to be all business most of the time."

"Does she have friends at Rolling Ridge?"

"She and Sue Evans seemed to be good friends, but I always wondered how you could be friends with your boss."

"You're not friends with Jim Rigby?" Ryan asked with a slight smirk.

"We get along okay, but I wouldn't call him a close friend."

"How does Sarah get along with Rigby?" Ryan asked.

"Fine, I guess. I've never seen them upset with each other or anything like that."

"What kind of guy is Rigby? Do you consider him a decent man?"

Jeb's eyes widened and his head tilted back.

"Decent? What do you mean?"

"What's most important to him--money, his employees, his customers?" Ryan asked.

"Not sure I know. I've never discussed it with him."

"You've worked for Rigby a long time. I'm sure you have an opinion. Just pick one," Ryan coaxed.

"I'd guess money. If he doesn't make money, we're all out of a job."

"Would he ever cheat to make more money?"

Jeb frowned, his body tensing. "I thought you were here to talk about Sarah."

"What do you think happened to Sarah?" Ryan asked quickly.

The question froze Jeb. His eyes went to Beth, then back to Ryan.

"I really don't know. I don't think anyone does," he replied, standing. "Say, I really need to get back to work. I've been painting my back door."

"Sure. I think we're done here," Ryan replied as he and Beth stood.

The two dogs frolicked in the front yard and Ryan called for Patches. The spaniel came running to Ryan's side before going to Jeb, circling his feet and sniffing.

"Come Patches!" Ryan ordered. "Get over here."

The inquisitive dog continued inspecting the lanky contractor's feet until Ryan reached over to grab his collar.

"Thanks for your time," Ryan said, leading Patches to his Bronco.

"I hope you get your painting done," Beth added. "The forecast is for rain later."

"I think it will hold off long enough," Jeb replied.

Patches leapt to the back seat before Ryan and Beth climbed inside. Jeb stood on the porch, watching as they backed out and drove away.

"So, what do you think?" Ryan asked.

"I didn't like the way he talked about Sarah in the past tense," she replied. "He was like the others. They all assume she's dead."

"I know what you mean. You'd think they'd at least be optimistic in front of us," Ryan said.

"Do you think he's involved in Sarah's disappearance?"

"I doubt it," Ryan replied. "He's such a simpleton. But I think he knows something."

"You know what else was weird?" Beth asked. "I didn't see one speck of paint on him."

- 7.3 -

"JEWELL, YOU DID GOOD THIS WEEKEND," J.D. told the dark-haired teen as she leaned half asleep against the passenger door of the pickup. Her diminutive body was consumed by the cavernous cab of the truck.

"Just give me a hit," she said, sitting up and turning her glazed eyes toward the driver. "I'm climbing outta my skin."

"We're a few minutes away. You can have all you want as soon as we get home," the stocky, bearded driver replied.

"Home? Is that what you call that place?" she sneered.

"It's shelter, food, and all the trinkets you've ever wanted," J.D. replied.

"When can I come and go on my own?" she asked. "I know other girls who do. You'd get your money either way."

"Stop running away, and we'll talk about it. I give you everything you want, and you still make me chase you down."

"I can handle myself," Jewell snapped. "I'll be eighteen soon, and nobody will be able to control my life--not you, not Daddy, nobody!"

"Dangerous men are out there looking for girls like you. I know the ones we can trust, the ones who pay big bucks. The other girls know what's good for them. You'll figure it out."

"Yeah, sure," she replied, turning away and leaning on the door.

J.D.'s cellphone chirped in the center console.

"What is it?" he asked.

"I'm thinking we should back off of Rigby. Pimping teenagers is one thing, but murder is completely another," his younger partner pleaded.

"What are you talking about? It was your idea to put the squeeze on Rigby."

"I don't know now," Slim said. "I guess I never thought it would lead to murder."

Jewell rotated her head around toward J.D.

"No one's been murdered," J.D. said, lowering his voice and turning from his young passenger.

"Who you talking to?" Jewell slurred. "Who's been murdered?"

"Nobody. Don't you worry about it," J.D. replied.

"Heather's murder is all over the news," Slim droned. "It's freakin' me out."

"Those drunken hunters were responsible for that. There's no way that gets pinned on us."

"There are people who know Heather worked for you! Someone will find out," Slim argued.

"Listen. Calm down. We're gonna follow through with the plan."

"What about Sarah Campbell? What's the plan for dealing with her?"

"She hasn't seen either one of us. We have plenty of options. Worst case, we'll pin whatever we decide on the fat real estate guy."

"Whatever we decide?" Slim shouted.

"Yeah. Whatever we decide."

FALLEN from SIGHT

- 7.4 -

THE THREE-INCH GASH ON THE BACK of Sarah's head was infected and warm to the touch, but there was little she could do.

It had been over a week since she'd been entombed in the twenty-foot square basement cell. She was unconscious when she'd been cast into the dark, dank basement, never getting a clear view of her masked captors. Sarah remembered going to Jefferson Peak, but little else, before waking up on the floor of the makeshift prison.

Four small windows butted against the ceiling in each corner of the cell. They each were boarded shut. Sunlight seeping through cracks provided the only way to tell day from night. Sarah had clawed and pulled at the boards for days without progress, leaving her fingertips blistered and bleeding.

Nothing had been left in the room that could be used for comfort or to aid in her escape. The floor was damp. The walls were barren. All light bulbs had been removed.

On the second day of her captivity, two masked men demanded she strip off her clothes in exchange for a stained grey sweatshirt, white painter's coveralls, and canvas tennis shoes that didn't come close to fitting.

With nothing but a cement floor for a bed, Sarah tore insulation from between the floor joists above and piled it in the corner of the room. The cushion allowed her to sleep, but the fiberglass worked its way into her scalp, face, and arms. Her skin was red and swollen. It itched and burned as if covered by fire ants.

A metal door leading upstairs was padlocked from the outside. She had passed through the opening only once, the day she was tossed inside the prison. Each evening since, her captor would arrive and exchange a bucket used as Sarah's toilet for a new pail, and an empty water bottle for one that was filled. On most nights, he'd also bring scraps of food.

Sarah used part of her drinking water to tend to her head wound and wash her face, but it did little to relieve the itching.

The man who appeared for the daily exchanges was stocky and average height. He wore a ski mask with a handgun stuck in his belt. He spoke with an unfamiliar voice. The only skin showing was his hands poking out of his long sleeve shirt. The dim light provided little opportunity to inspect her captor, but the hands were those of an outdoorsman or a construction worker—strong, tan, and callused.

On occasion, Sarah heard footsteps and voices above, but she couldn't make out the conversations. It wasn't clear if anyone lived in the house, but she didn't think so. Most of the time it was eerily quiet.

She waited each morning until she was sure no one was in the building, and then she'd call for help. But no one ever came. She occasionally heard the faint sounds of a car or truck passing in the distance, but they were too far away to hear her pleas.

Sarah's stomach rumbled as she sat staring at the bucket of her waste beside the door. It was well past the normal time for the exchange, but no sounds came from above.

FALLEN from SIGHT

The room reeked of urine and feces. There was no place to escape the odor in the damp cell that had become Sarah's universe.

Hunger, loneliness, and fear filled her days, but she refused to give up.

Ryan will come. I know Ryan will come.

.

- Day 8 -

RYAN SAT IN THE LIVING ROOM watching Channel 7 News out of Boone when Beth awoke. She lumbered down the hall from the guest room in a long, white bathrobe, her hair piled atop her head.

"Anything new this morning?" she asked.

"Nothing. It's like the investigation into Sarah's disappearance has stalled," Ryan replied. "They're way more focused on the Jane Doe case."

"How so?"

"Apparently, dozens of parents have come forward wanting information on their missing redheaded teenage daughters."

"I feel terrible for the poor victim, but nothing can be done to save her. Sarah's still out there. I can feel it."

"The media's trying to tie the cases together," Ryan said. "I just heard a so-called investigative expert say, 'Find the Jane Doe killer and you'll find Sarah Campbell.' It makes me want to scream."

"These cops clearly need some help," Beth said. "I thought you told me this guy from Charlotte was solid."

"Detective Baker? Yeah. I looked him up. His résumé's impressive."

"You want a refill?" Beth asked. "I need some caffeine in my body."

"No, I've had plenty."

Beth quickly returned and took a seat at the far end of the sofa.

"Of all the people we've talked with, Jeb Jones seemed the most suspicious. I'm certain he wasn't shooting straight with us," Beth said.

"Yeah. He definitely seemed different than when I'd worked with him in the past."

"Should we go to the police and see if they'll look into what he's up to?" Beth asked.

"Based on what? We didn't exactly come up with hard evidence."

"He was clearly nervous when we asked him what he thought happened to Sarah. He practically kicked us out, and he was lying about painting, unless he's the neatest painter in the Southeast."

"That's not enough to go to the cops. Williams and Phillips would throw us out on our butts," Ryan replied.

"Then what? We've met with everyone on my list with the exception of a couple of contractors."

Ryan paused, staring at the TV.

"Let's go back and see Rigby," he said. "We can dig a little deeper into what he knows about Jones' activities—both at and away from work."

"Fine with me," Beth replied. "I'll get dressed. We can grab breakfast on the way."

Ryan's face turned solemn, and he clasped his hands.

"Say, wait a second," he said, standing. "There's something I've wanted to tell you for a few days, but I haven't found the right time."

"That look is scaring me. What is it, Ryan?"

"No one knows what I'm about to say. Sarah wanted to tell you in person, but she never got that chance," Ryan said, his voice wavering.

Beth took a deep breath and sat down, crossing her arms.

"Don't tell me Sarah's expecting."

"No, but you're close," Ryan replied. "We're engaged. She accepted my proposal the last night we were together. I'd made a reservation at Chetola Lodge for Saturday night to celebrate."

"Oh my God," Beth squealed, wrapping her arms around Ryan. "That's fantastic!"

Ryan and Beth stepped back. He wiped his eyes before Beth could notice.

"She wanted to be the one to let you know and show you her ring," Ryan said. "I was waiting until we found Sarah, but I thought we both needed a lift today."

"I'm glad you told me," Beth said. "But shouldn't you've informed the police? Maybe she was kidnapped for her ring."

"Beth, I'm a carpenter. It's a nice ring, but I promised Sarah to get her a larger diamond someday."

Beth chuckled. "I'm going to love having you in the family. Unless you have more news, I'm going to get ready to go see Rigby."

FALLEN from SIGHT

- 8.1 -

JAMES RIGBY STRODE past his assistant seated at her desk, his eyes focused straight ahead.

"Marge, no interruptions this morning," he barked before disappearing into his office and slamming the door.

He took his cellphone from his pocket and slid it to the center of the desk before removing his jacket and flopping into his chair. After two nights with little sleep, he looked like an inmate awaiting execution. His furrowed brow protruded over sunken, red eyes.

He sat staring at his cellphone as if it were a time bomb ready to explode. The call from his blackmailer could come at any second. Too nervous to wait, Rigby reached for the phone and dialed Jack Spathe.

At the other end, the greasy-haired loan shark pulled the cigar stub from his mouth and looked at the caller ID. Before answering, he took a final sip from his coffee mug.

"First you call me on a Saturday, and now you interrupt my Monday morning coffee," Spathe said. "This better be good."

"Jack, you gotta come through for me on this! I need the money today."

"Today? I told you Wednesday was the best I could do, and frankly, I'm not sure that's possible. One mil in unmarked bills is no easy errand. I'm calling in favors with my Vegas contacts to pull this off."

"I'm telling you this business deal will go south if I don't have the money today," Rigby pleaded.

"Jimbo, we both know this ain't no bidness deal. My guess is you either have your tit in a wringer wit one of your ex-wives, or someone's dug up dirt on one of your development projects. Either way, you're not gettin' no cash today."

"How much *could* you get today?" Rigby asked, his voice dripping with desperation.

The line was silent for a long moment.

"Maybe fifty G's. That would be the most," Spathe replied. "And it'll cost ya thirty percent, not twenty."

"Fine. Where can I meet you to pick it up?"

"You're gonna need ta come ta Charlotte. I don't have time to drive up ta the mountains," Spathe replied.

"How about one of your guys meeting me halfway? Maybe at the rest stop on I-77. We've met there before."

"Yeah. I guess I could arrange that. Be there at noon, and don't be late!"

Rigby placed the phone on the desk and leaned back in his chair as his office door cracked open and Marge's fretful face appeared.

"I know you said no interruptions, but Ryan Nelson says it's important that he see you. He's with Sarah's sister."

Rigby glanced down at his Rolex. It was 9:35.

"Tell them I'm swamped. Maybe later in the week."

"Okay," Marge replied, backing out of the doorway.

"Wait!" Rigby called. "I can spare ten minutes, but no more."

He surveyed the tops of his desk and credenza. Finding everything in order, he pulled a random file from his drawer, placed it on the desk, and began leafing through it.

"Mr. Rigby, thanks for agreeing to meet with us," Ryan said as he and Beth stepped into the office.

"I only have a few minutes, but please have a seat," Rigby said. "I'm glad you came by. I've been wondering how you've been doing. Any news on Sarah?"

"Actually, no," Beth replied. "The lack of information from Parsons Creek PD has been frustrating."

"We miss her around here. She's a hard worker, and liked by everyone. A real positive team member."

Ryan turned to Beth with raised eyebrows.

"We stopped by to talk to Jeb Jones the other day, and ..."

"Say, before we get into that," Rigby interrupted, "I had something I wanted to ask you when you were here a couple of days ago."

"What's that?" Ryan asked.

"We talked about the faulty soil tests that were corrected," Rigby began.

"Yeah. I remember. What about it?"

"Did Sarah ever mention talking to Fred Warren about the tests?" Rigby asked.

"No. I can't say I recall her ever mentioning that name. Why do you ask?"

"Fred said he was asked about the initial tests several weeks ago by a young woman claiming to work at Rolling Ridge," Rigby lied. "I'm just trying to find out who that may have been."

"If this happened several weeks ago, why didn't you ask Sarah then?" Ryan asked.

Rigby paused.

"Uh… It just came up a few days ago when I was talking with Warren about the phase two tests."

"What's your concern?" Ryan asked. "I thought the initial tests were corrected."

"Yeah. They were. I was just curious if it was Sarah talking to Warren, plus I don't want any false information floating around."

Ryan looked to Beth, then back to Rigby.

"Can I get back to why Beth and I came here today?" Ryan asked.

"Sure. Go ahead."

Before Ryan could begin, Rigby's cellphone rang on his desk. Ryan and Rigby looked at the phone. *Unknown Caller* was displayed on the screen.

"I'm sorry. I need to take this. We'll have to meet later in the week."

"We can wait in the lobby," Ryan suggested.

"Sorry. I'm out of time today. Please shut the door on your way out."

Rigby reached for the phone with one hand and pointed to the office door with the other. Ryan and Beth stood and quickly left the room, continuing across the lobby and out the front of the building.

"What do you think *that* was all about?" Beth asked.

"As soon as we entered, Rigby was as nervous as a cat in a room full of pit bulls," Ryan replied. "All he seemed to care about were those soil tests."

"There's definitely something fishy going on," Beth said. "We don't have anything specific, but we can't sit on this. Let's go find Detective Phillips."

"YOUR TIME IS UP, RIGBY," J.D.'s muffled voice said. "Bring the money to the Boone UPS store on Mountain View Road at exactly three p.m. The key to PO box one twenty-three is under your driver side mat."

"What? My car's been with me all weekend."

"Shut up and listen!" J.D. shouted. "We'll be watching. Don't bring anyone else. Any mistakes and you'll be looking through prison bars before tomorrow morning."

"But I couldn't get all the…," Rigby stuttered.

"Be there at three!"

"You don't understand. I need more time."

Rigby spoke into a dead line, his final words unheard.

He looked at his watch. It was a two-hour drive to pick up the cash at the I-77 rest area and then another two-hour drive back up to Boone.

He was out of time.

THE BLACKMAILER made the call to Rigby from an empty rest area pavilion off I-421, a fifteen-minute drive to Parsons Creek. The stocky, square-jawed J.D. stuffed the throwaway cellphone back into his pants pocket.

"Do you think he has the cash?" Slim asked, puffing on a cigarette.

"He'd better. I've got too much going on to mess around with that fat bastard," J.D. replied. "We need to pick up another girl tonight. She's at Victor County Corrections."

"That place is a hellhole. The worst in Tennessee," Slim replied.

"It sure is, and she's facing her second opioid possession charge. She'll be glad to get out."

"Victor County is more than three hours from here. Are you sure we have time for both the pickup and springing the girl?"

J.D. frowned.

"Why don't you make the Tennessee trip?" he asked. "I can handle the pickup in Boone."

Slim threw his cigarette to the floor and angrily snuffed it out with his toe.

"I take all the risks bailing out these girls," he snapped. "And I'm only getting twenty percent of what they bring in."

"We agreed that you'd bail out the girls. You're the one with fake IDs and the hometown look. Who's gonna question that baby face?"

"Then I should get at least half of the Rigby money," the lanky man protested. "It was my idea."

J.D.'s eyes narrowed as he took two steps toward his partner. The slighter built man shuffled back.

"Listen, Slim! I'm the one who brought you into this business. It's me who molds these girls and makes sure they stay in line. I find the johns who pay big bucks and come back again and again," the fire-eyed trafficker shouted, pushing his finger into the breastbone of his partner. "Just do what you're told, and be happy you don't have to live off the scraps your day job pays."

Slim pushed away his partner's hand and stepped back.

"It's late. I need to get to work before someone wonders where I went," Slim said.

"You do that. I'll pick up the money at three and text you the details on the Tennessee girl," J.D. replied. "I'll expect you to have her at my place tonight."

- 8.2 -

RYAN CALLED TO MAKE SURE Detective Phillips would be in his office, but reached his voicemail greeting. The message said he'd return in the early afternoon. After lunch, Ryan and Beth drove silently to downtown Parsons Creek with far-off stares on their tired faces.

They circled the two-story redbrick courthouse at the center of the square with its white stone columns bracketing the entrance. The police station was on the square's northeast corner. Ryan pulled his Bronco to a stop at a visitor space near the entrance where news crews were hovering with cameras and microphones at the ready.

"Just look straight ahead and keep moving," Ryan said.

They walked quickly and stepped around the reporters, pushing aside their outstretched mics.

Detective Phillips was waiting in the lobby, reading email on his iPhone, when Ryan and Beth entered. Phillips quickly ushered them to the privacy of a conference room.

"What's so urgent that you couldn't cover this on the phone?" Phillips asked.

"We've been meeting with people who work with Sarah," Ryan began, "and we're concerned with what we've heard from James Rigby."

Phillips crossed his arms.

"You're continuing your amateur investigation even after I warned of the danger? Your interference could hamper our efforts!"

Beth bristled. "I can't see that we're *hampering* your efforts," she shot back. "In fact, it's hard to tell that you're making *any* effort. It's been over a week, and you have zero suspects."

"And you've given us no feedback," Ryan added. "From what we see on TV, all your focus is on the Jane Doe case."

Phillips leaned back, staring down his nose at the frustrated couple, appearing to weigh his response.

"It's no longer the Jane Doe case," he replied. "Her name is Heather McCoy. We matched the victim's DNA to a seventeen-year-old girl from southeast Kentucky who'd been missing more than a year."

"Seventeen?" Beth gasped, turning to Ryan.

"Yeah. Detective Baker has contacted Kentucky authorities and they've met with the victim's parents," Phillips replied. "The FBI is involved now."

"It's good to see progress on the murder case, but Sarah's out there somewhere. What's being done to find her?" Ryan asked.

"It's possible the two cases are linked, so progress on the murder investigation may eventually lead us to Sarah," Phillips argued.

"That sounds like a long shot to me," Ryan replied, "and in the meantime, Sarah's life could be in jeopardy."

"Okay. So, tell me. What do you junior detectives have for me this afternoon?"

"Rigby's hiding something," Ryan said. "We're convinced of it."

"Something? That's pretty vague," Phillips scoffed. "Can you be more specific?"

"It has something to do with the county soil tests at the Rolling Ridge development," Ryan said. "More than once he's brought up the subject and asked if Sarah discussed it with me."

"That's it?" Phillips asked. "He's asked you what Sarah told you about soil tests?"

"We've also learned that he searched Sarah's desk shortly after she disappeared, looking for a customer file that didn't exist. I think he was looking for something else."

"I was aware that he and Sue Evans searched Sarah's desk, but nothing was removed," Phillips said.

"Sue called me the other day looking for Sarah's notepad," Ryan continued. "She told me she had to step away for a phone call when Rigby searched the desk. I think she's suspicious of him, too."

Phillips stood.

"This all makes for great theater, but it's total speculation. No one else has come forward with anything indicating James Rigby is involved in this missing person's case. Now if you don't mind, I need to get back to work."

Ryan and Beth scowled up at Phillips. As they began to stand, a knock came to the door.

"Just a minute," Phillips said, signaling for them to stay seated.

He stepped to the door and pulled it open to find Mike Arnold, a junior patrolman, standing on the other side.

"What is it?"

The young officer looked up at the tall detective and took a deep breath.

"I was staffing the public hotline, and I just received a suspicious call."

"Go see Williams. He's triaging those calls," Phillips said.

"I already did. Williams said it was probably just some crackpot, but that I should inform you anyway."

Phillips closed the conference room door and stepped into the hall closer to the nervous patrolman.

"What did the caller say?"

"He said that he had proof James Rigby bribed the county soil and water inspector and that the Rolling Ridge development was in violation of North Carolina septic restrictions."

Phillips turned and stared back at the conference room where Ryan and Beth sat waiting.

"What proof?"

"He didn't say."

"Did this guy say anything else?"

"He said we should check Rigby's basement. What we find there will break the Campbell case wide open."

- 8.3 -

JAMES RIGBY PULLED his black Escalade off the county road and onto the winding lane leading to his house. The sun set to his rear as he followed the shadow of his vehicle toward several police cars parked in front of his expansive home.

Recognizing Detective Phillips' cruiser, his heart rate spiked. He navigated around the police vehicles and parked in his driveway.

Three uniformed officers, Phillips, and Baker waited at the front porch, their faces as solemn as pallbearers.

The portly real estate developer slid from his SUV and stepped cautiously up the sidewalk toward the greeting party.

"I hope this doesn't mean my cat set off the house alarm again," Rigby said, forcing a smile.

The lawmen remained stoic.

"I have a warrant for your arrest," Phillips said, stepping forward and flashing a document.

"You can't be serious. For what?"

Sgt. Williams read Rigby his rights as another patrolman pulled the suspect's hands behind him and applied handcuffs.

"At least tell me what I'm accused of doing," Rigby pleaded.

"For now, you're charged with bribing a county official and violating state water and sewer restrictions," Phillips said.

"That's ridiculous! I have certificates of inspection from the county. Who's feeding you this B.S.?"

"Save your breath, Rigby. We just spoke with Fred Warren. He sang like a bird. You'll be occupying the cell next to his tonight."

"Warren's confused," Rigby protested. "He's been under a lot of pressure with his wife's cancer. The money I offered him was to help pay her medical bills."

Phillips shook his head, sneering.

"Try to maintain some shred of dignity, Rigby. Keep your mouth shut until you get a lawyer."

"Give me your house keys!" a patrolman ordered.

"Do you have a search warrant? You can't just burst into my house," Rigby argued.

"Here's the document," Phillips said, pulling it from his sport coat and sticking it in the prisoner's face. "The process doesn't take long in Birch County."

"You won't find anything in my house except my cat. Someone better take care of Reggie!" he demanded.

"Your keys," the patrolman repeated, extending his hand, palm up.

"They're in my SUV, but you're wasting your time."

"You'd better hope we are," Baker said. "Bribing a public official is only five to ten. Murder will get you a lifetime stay at Raleigh Central."

"Murder? You guys are nuts!" Rigby shouted as he was dragged to a waiting police car. "I'm being framed!"

The uniformed officer found the keys in the SUV and unlocked the front door to Rigby's home, while Sgt. Williams and another officer drove Rigby back to Parsons Creek Police Department.

Phillips, Baker and the remaining officers pulled on disposable shoe covers and latex gloves before entering the front hallway.

Phillips flipped on the ceiling lights as Rigby's oversized feline came stalking down the hall from the living room.

"Jesus, what was that?" a patrolman asked, taking a step back.

"I guess Rigby does everything on a grand scale," Phillips said before shooing the cat further back into the house.

Phillips stepped down the hall and past the living room with the other two officers following.

"This isn't your average Parsons Creek home," Phillips said, stopping to study the rooms.

The house was richly appointed with the finest furnishings and accents. Everything appeared untouched and spotless, looking more like a series of showrooms at an upscale furniture store than a home someone actually inhabited.

"How do you get to the basement?" Phillips asked. "Do you guys see any stairs?"

"Over there," Baker said, shining his flashlight toward a spiral staircase at the back of the family room.

The staircase wound downward to a large recreation room, complete with wet bar, pool table, several arcade games, and an eight-foot-wide TV screen. The walkout basement had a wall of windows and sliding glass doors overlooking the backyard.

The lawmen spread out and inspected the sprawling man cave, looking under and around furniture, behind the wet bar, even inside the refrigerator.

Phillips opened a door leading to another room in the basement. The room was as dark as a coal mine shaft. Phillips felt around the wall on the inside and flipped on a light switch. The unfinished cinderblock room contained the home's mechanical systems—furnace, water heaters, and a control panel for the security system.

Phillips pulled a penlight from his pocket and shined it behind the furnace. A lone paint can, appearing out of place, rested in the far corner against the wall. Phillips squeezed around the furnace to retrieve it.

Shaking the sealed can produced a muffled rattle. He took a Swiss Army knife from his pocket and wedged the can between his legs. He then slid the knife blade around the edge of the lid, gradually loosening it. With one final twist of the blade, the lid popped off. A black bra and silk panties dropped to the cement floor.

"In here!" Phillips shouted.

Baker and the patrolmen sprinted toward his voice. They stopped short and stared as Phillips held up the bra between his gloved forefinger and thumb.

"Looks like James Rigby has some explaining to do," he said.

- 8.4 -

IT TOOK LONGER than Slim expected to arrange bail for Shari Yontz, the wisp of a woman held inside the eastern Tennessee jailhouse. Even though her driver's license claimed the blue-eyed blonde with a Tweety Bird tattoo on her left ankle was twenty, Sheriff Blake Winkler wasn't convinced. He demanded proof she wasn't a minor. He called Slim to the courthouse to ask him a few questions.

Slim found the stern-faced sheriff in his office seated behind his desk. Resembling Jack Nicholson from *A Few Good Men*, the rural lawman was in formal uniform with his saucer hat placed on the corner of his desk. The shiny black bill and gold sheriff's emblem faced forward.

"You asked to see me?" Slim inquired, sticking his head through the crack in the door.

"I don't *ask*," the crusty sheriff replied, not looking up. "I *told* you to come."

"Well, I'm here. How can I help you?" he asked, walking to the front of Winkler's desk.

"You're a cocky little fart, aren't you?" the sheriff barked.

"No, sir. I'm not cocky, and I'm well over six feet tall."

Winkler's neck glowed red. "I could fine you and toss your ass in jail for contempt of court," he growled.

Slim paused.

"I'm sorry, sir. It's been a long day, and I didn't realize this was a courtroom. I'll be glad to answer any questions."

The sheriff coughed into his clenched fist to clear his throat.

"I think this girl's a minor, and I can't just turn her over to anyone off the street. I'll need a family member to sign for her."

"I understand," Slim replied. "But I've been told she's twenty."

"How do you know this girl?" the sheriff asked.

"Her father sent me to bail her out."

"You don't look like anyone from Rocky Falls. I hunt up that way. I can guaran-damn-tee you that those folks don't wear sport coats or own gold watches."

"Well, actually her father contacted a friend of mine. He was busy, so he sent me to bail her out."

"What's your friend's name? Is he from around here?"

Slim paused. J.D. had made it clear he didn't want to be connected with bailing out any of the girls.

"No, sir. I doubt if you'd know him. He served with the girl's father in Desert Storm."

The sheriff studied Slim, digesting his answer.

"You think you could get her daddy down here?"

"Uh. I don't know for sure. I can try."

"I'll give you an hour. No more. I've already had a long day."

Slim stepped out of the room and into the outer hallway to place his call.

"Shit! Can't you do anything?" J.D. bellowed after getting the news.

"He gave me an hour, and I have a feeling if I don't produce the girl's father, the sheriff's going to keep asking questions."

"Sit tight, and don't piss off this backwoods cop more than you already have."

FORTY-FIVE MINUTES LATER, a middle-aged man with a three-month-old crewcut, wearing jeans, a camo tee shirt, and a Titans ball cap, entered the front of the courthouse. As he approached, the smell of whiskey and aftershave lotion grew more intense.

"You the bail guy?" the bewhiskered man asked.

"Yes. Are you Mr. Yontz?"

"Damned straight. I'm Shari's daddy. J.D. said you'd have an extra hundred for me."

"Once I get your daughter bailed out, I'll get you the cash. Are you okay to talk to the sheriff?" Slim asked.

"Sure. I'm fine."

"The sheriff will want to see your ID. He'll ask if your daughter is older than eighteen and if it's okay for me to bail her out."

"No problem. The little bitch owes me. The wife and I have been takin' care of her screamin' rug rat near on a year."

IT WAS APPROACHING MIDNIGHT when Slim pulled off I-221 and guided his dark sedan north toward J.D.'s twenty-acre compound.

Two hundred yards ahead, the headlights flashed across J.D. stepping out the back of a small aging cabin. He was carrying a stainless steel pail which he took to the edge of the woods, tossing its contents into the wild shrubs.

"What's goin' on down there?" the weary girl asked.

"Pray you never find out," Slim replied, pulling into the driveway of J.D.'s two-story home.

Shari's drug-induced expression didn't change as her head rotated toward the impressive residence.

"Is this where I'll be stayin'?"

"Yeah. You'll have your own room and most everything else you'll need," Slim said.

"You stay here, too?" she asked.

"No. I have a job and a house closer to town."

"That's too bad," she replied.

J.D. walked up the lane from the cabin toward Slim's car.

"Stay here for a minute. I need to talk to J.D," Slim instructed as he slid from the sedan.

"You're feeding her a little late tonight. How's she doin'?" Slim asked.

"She's alive if that's what you're askin', but it ain't gonna matter much longer," J.D. replied.

"Not matter? What do you mean?"

"Rigby's in jail. The cops must've found what we planted in his basement. He's been charged with kidnapping, and once they find her body, it'll be changed to murder."

"I thought you said after we got the money, we'd turn Sarah loose," Slim said, panic in his eyes.

"The asshole only came up with fifty thousand. He deserves a life sentence."

"Sarah's never seen us. Why kill her?" Slim pleaded.

"She knows two men are holding her," J.D. replied. "Rigby would need to have a partner. Otherwise, how could Rigby release her after he was arrested?"

Slim stared at J.D., his mind racing.

"You'd always planned to kill her, didn't you?" Slim asked, his voice rising in anger.

"And if you get in the way, I won't hesitate to put a bullet in your head, too," J.D. growled. "I can find someone else to bail out these girls.

"Let's get Blondie inside, and then you get your ass back home. Cops are gonna be crawling all over Parsons Creek now that they have Rigby behind bars. You need to be as surprised as everyone else tomorrow."

"What are you going to do with the body?" Slim asked.

"I haven't decided, but I don't have much time."

"Why's that?"

"They'll be able to tell how long she's been dead," J.D. replied.

"What if you put the body where they'll never find it? Then there's no rush to kill her," Slim said.

"Maybe, but she's sure as hell not serving any purpose alive."

FALLEN from SIGHT

- Day 9 -

"I'M BEING FRAMED," James Rigby pleaded.

The late morning interrogation with the real estate developer was in its fourth hour. Wearing his newly issued orange jumpsuit, Rigby's eyes were bloodshot and sunken into his sagging face. A sleepless night and the grilling from Phillips and Baker were taking their toll.

Victor Manson, Rigby's real estate attorney, had arranged for Theresa Barrett to represent him. The 55-year-old defense attorney from Charlotte had represented the worst criminals the Queen City had to offer, freeing many of them.

Barrett sat next to Rigby. Presenting an all-business demeanor, the middle-aged brunette kept her eyes focused on Phillips.

"My client's conceding that he bribed a county official, but the charges of kidnapping and murder are unfounded and lack evidence," Barrett argued.

"Then how do you explain Sarah Campbell's underwear in his basement?" Phillips asked. "Blood samples confirmed the items belong to the missing woman."

"Whoever was blackmailing him must've placed the clothes inside his home," Barrett replied. "He's told you several times the blackmailer threatened to frame him with murder if he didn't deliver the million dollars. It was after Mr. Rigby failed to deliver the required amount that these clothes showed up and the hotline received the anonymous tip."

Phillips leaned toward Detective Baker, shielding his mouth with his hand. Baker nodded in approval to whatever Phillips told him.

"Here's what really happened," Phillips said, turning to Rigby. "You got wind that the Campbell girl was going to blow the whistle on your arrangement with Fred Warren. You envisioned your multimillion-dollar development crashing down on your head, so you killed her."

"That's ridiculous!" Barrett shouted. "Did he then call the hotline and tell the cops where to find the victim's underwear?"

"Mr. Rigby must have had an accomplice who got cold feet and wanted him to take the fall," Phillips replied firmly.

"Your hypothesis is getting more ridiculous," Barrett said, tossing her hands in the air. "What motive would this other person have to kill the Campbell girl?"

"The same motive as James Rigby: to keep her quiet about the soil tests."

"Are you accusing Fred Warren of blackmailing my client and framing him for murder?" she asked.

"Warren has already proven to be a crooked public servant," Phillips said. "It's not a stretch to think he'd be greedy enough to put the squeeze on Rigby one more time."

"What is Warren saying?" Barrett asked.

"He's denying any knowledge of the murder and any role in blackmailing Rigby, but would you expect anything else?"

Barrett turned her piercing blue-eyed stare toward Detective Baker.

"I'd expect this half-assed police work from a backwoods police force. They come across a murder about as often as Halley's Comet appears. But surely someone with twenty-plus years at Charlotte Homicide can see how preposterous this sounds."

"The DA has plans to impanel a grand jury based on the evidence we have," Baker replied.

"So, you think two middle-aged men with one traffic ticket between them woke up one morning and decided to kill an innocent woman?" she asked, her stare intensifying.

"Desperate men will do desperate things," Baker calmly replied. "Their careers were in the balance if Ms. Campbell went to the police."

"Well, good luck in court. You have no body, no witnesses, and clothes that could have been planted by anyone," Barrett said, standing. "My client has cooperated on the charges of bribery, but we're through here today if you insist on pursuing this ridiculous murder/blackmail scenario."

Phillips stood and stepped to the door where two patrolmen waited outside.

"Take the prisoner back to his cell," Phillips ordered. "We're done in here."

Barrett glared at Baker as her client was led from the room.

"You and I both know Rigby didn't do this," she said.

BAKER FOLLOWED PHILLIPS down the hall to his office beside Chief Adkins' conference room. They both flopped down in chairs, exhausted from the four-hour interrogation.

"There's a chance Rigby's telling the truth," Baker began, "and that he was being blackmailed by someone who knew he'd bribed Warren."

"Who knew other than Rigby and Warren, and apparently Sarah Campbell?" Phillips asked.

"It's hard for three people to keep a secret. Maybe someone else found out," Baker suggested.

"There's no evidence to support that theory, and we have plenty of evidence pointing to Rigby and Warren. Plus, they had a clear motive for killing the girl," Phillips said.

"If Rigby's telling the truth, then there's a kidnapper and blackmailer still out there. There's also a chance Sarah Campbell's still alive."

"Don't be sharing that B.S. with the press!" Phillips shouted. "We already have Heather McCoy's killer on the loose. Don't go scaring the public by saying Sarah Campbell's kidnapper is still walking around Parsons Creek."

Baker stood and looked down at Phillips. "I'll not go public with the possibilities, but I'll damned well continue to investigate both cases."

FALLEN from SIGHT

- 9.1 -

IT TOOK LESS THAN TWENTY-FOUR HOURS for the news of James Rigby's arrest to spread across Parsons Creek, as well as the entire state. News crews could be seen everywhere seeking details and more dirt on the accused killer.

"I REFUSE TO BELIEVE SARAH'S DEAD," Ryan said as he sat watching the noon news with Patches at his feet. "It seems everyone's already convicted Rigby and begun the search for Sarah's body."

"You don't think Rigby's guilty?" Beth asked, taking a seat on the sofa.

"Sure, of bribing a county inspector. But I'm not ready to convict him of murder."

"Then what do you think happened?"

"I think someone who didn't care much for Rigby found out about his bribery scheme from Sarah, and she ended up in the middle of it," Ryan replied.

"Do you really believe that's what happened?"

"I have to, because if the cops are right and Rigby's guilty, then Sarah's probably dead. At least with my theory, there's a chance we can still find her."

"But the cops have quit looking for a killer," Beth said.

"Then we'll need to keep looking on our own. All roads lead to Rolling Ridge. I think we need to get back out there and gauge the reaction to Rigby's arrest, starting with his foreman."

CABLE NEWS VANS congested the Rolling Ridge parking lot. Signs had been posted at the entrance to the lot stating the offices were closed until further notice, but the signs did little to dissuade reporters.

Sue Evans and Lance Baldwin had locked themselves inside the sales office, and Jeb Jones and Rigby's assistant, Marge Jackson, were holding down the fort at the management office.

"All these phone calls are driving me nuts," Lance said as Sue Evans stepped toward his desk. "We can't keep telling clients we'll call back. They want to know if their homes will be finished, or if they'll get their deposits back."

"I don't know what to tell them. I still can't get over Jim being arrested for Sarah's disappearance. It's all so crazy," Sue said, taking a seat across from Lance.

"I don't know Rigby as well as you, but I always had a feeling the guy was a little sleazy," Lance said.

"Sleazy is one thing, but murder's another. I never in a million years would expect he could do such a thing."

"Not everyone is as they seem," Lance said.

"That's a frightening analysis."

"Even you were suspicious of his motives for searching Sarah's desk," Lance argued.

"Yeah, but I never suspected all this. It's beyond believable."

"What are you hearing from over at the management office?"

"I just talked to Jeb. He said that he and Marge are fending off contractor calls, asking if and when they'll get paid," Sue replied. "Marge put a call in to one of the Charlotte investors to get a reading, and he said the operational funds would be frozen until he and the other investors could determine the cost of getting the sanitary systems back within code."

"That could take months," Lance said, standing and patting his pockets before pulling out a pack of cigarettes.

"Do you mind if I smoke in here? It would be suicide to go out there right now."

"I didn't know you smoked," Sue replied.

"I started again recently."

RYAN SQUEEZED HIS FORD BRONCO around the news vans and found a parking spot near the front of the Rolling Ridge management office. He and Beth were immediately recognized. Reporters came running as questions rang out.

"What brings you to Rolling Ridge?"

"Do you think Rigby killed your sister?"

"Should he get the death penalty?"

Ryan put one arm around Beth and held out the other as he forced his way to the entrance of the management office. He pounded twice on the locked front door.

"Looks like Sarah's sister and Ryan Nelson," Jones said as he peeked out the front window. "Should I let them in?"

"Do they look angry?" Marge asked.

"No, not really."

"Then I don't see any harm in letting them in," she replied. "We've got nothing to hide."

Jones unlocked the door, and Ryan and Beth squeezed inside, holding back the reporters.

"I thought I answered all your questions the other day," Jones said.

"That was before your boss was arrested," Ryan replied. "We'd like to get your view as to what's happened. Did you see this coming?"

"Hell, no," Marge replied from behind her desk. "If I had, I'd have been out looking for another job."

"What about you? Did you think your boss was capable of murder?" Ryan asked, turning to Jones.

"He's a tough businessman, maybe even stretched the rules a bit. But a killer? No way."

"Did you know he bribed Fred Warren?" Ryan asked.

"He never told me, if that's what you're asking," Jones replied, furrowing his brow. "He didn't share much inside information about the business. I was his operations guy. He told me just enough to keep things moving."

"Surely you suspected something was going on," Ryan said.

"Listen! I can see where you're going, and I didn't blackmail my boss!" Jones bellowed.

"You're his assistant," Beth said, turning to Marge. "Did you know what was going on with Warren?"

"No! That son of a bitch treated me like a slave. I had my job to do, and that was it," she replied. "In the five years I've worked for Rigby, he never so much as took me to lunch."

Ryan looked to Beth. His shoulder shrug was the signal to move on.

"How do people around here view Sarah?" Beth asked. "She came with the sales team a few years back. Did she fit in?"

"She was sure good to look at," Jones said. "The best-looking woman I'd seen in a while. No offense, Marge."

"None taken," Marge grunted.

"All the younger guys talked about asking her out, but we all figured she was out of our league," Jones said.

"Did *you* ever ask her for a date?" Ryan asked, his face tensing.

Jones smirked.

"Who, me? She never gave me the time of day. I was just someone to do her favors. Besides, at first, I thought she and Lance Baldwin were a couple."

"How do you mean?" Ryan asked.

"They often had lunch together. They were always smiling and kidding each other. You know. Couple stuff."

"Sarah never mentioned Lance Baldwin to me," Beth said. "And we discussed everything, especially boyfriends."

"I guess I wasn't reading it right," Jones said, turning to Ryan. "It makes little difference now. After you started showing up, everyone figured she was taken."

"You figured right," Ryan said.

"Someone around here must've known what was going on between Rigby and Warren," Beth said. "You have to admit you two are the most likely candidates. If not you, then who?"

Marge looked toward Jones. His head shake was barely noticeable.

"We don't have a clue," Marge said.

"Thanks for your time," Ryan said. "Could you do us a favor and call the sales office so they can let us in?"

"Sure," Marge replied.

Beth and Ryan walked back toward the entrance. The cameras and reporters were several rows deep outside the door.

"You think we can make it across that parking lot in one piece?" Beth asked.

"Follow me," Ryan said as he opened the door and leaned into the shouting throng.

One reporter made the mistake of stepping in front of Ryan, blocking his path to the sidewalk. The 190-pound former high school linebacker pushed the belligerent newsman to the ground like he was cutting through an offensive line.

Sue Evans and Lance Baldwin met them at the entrance, and Lance shut the door immediately after they entered.

"I didn't expect to see you back out here again," Sue said. "Not after Rigby was arrested."

"We're not giving up until we find Sarah," Beth said, "and there are still too many unanswered questions."

"Like what?" Lance asked. "What I heard on the news this morning sounded pretty cut and dried."

"Does Fred Warren look like the kinda guy who could kill a young woman and then blackmail a real estate tycoon like Rigby?" Ryan asked.

"Not really," Sue replied, "but he *did* accept a bribe from Rigby."

"Accepting a bribe is a passive crime, something that would be hard for some people to turn down. Killing someone and then instigating a blackmail scheme is way above anything a county inspector like Fred Warren is capable of doing," Ryan argued.

"Maybe Rigby killed her, and Warren just took advantage of the situation," Lance suggested.

"That's possible, I guess," Ryan replied, "but I still don't see James Rigby as a killer, nor can I envision Warren cooking up a blackmail scheme on his own."

"Then what's your theory?" Lance asked.

"I think Sarah made the mistake of telling someone about the soil test cover-up, which led to her being kidnapped and held as part of a blackmail plan."

"Who could she have told?" Sue asked. "And why wouldn't she just go to the police?"

"I don't have all the answers," Ryan replied. "Maybe she wasn't totally convinced of what Rigby was doing, and she was looking for more information."

"That would imply it was someone she trusted," Sue added.

"Possibly," Ryan replied, turning to Lance. "Didn't you say Sarah asked you once if you trusted Jeb Jones?"

"Yeah, but I have no idea if it was about this. That's a huge assumption to make," Lance replied.

"Maybe, but if my theory's correct, someone Sarah knows is behind her disappearance," Ryan said.

"So why are you here to see us?" Sue asked. "Surely, you don't think her coworkers are involved."

Ryan paused.

"Were you ever in a relationship with Sarah?" he asked.

"That's ridiculous," Lance replied, frowning. "Who told you that?"

"When you first came here, Jeb said he thought you and Sarah were a couple."

Lance's body tensed. His hands tightened into fists.

"That Appalachian hillbilly's probably never been with a woman. How would he even know what a couple looked like?" Lance roared, rage in his eyes.

"Is that a no?" Ryan asked.

"Ask Sue. We were friends, but that was it!"

Sue stared at Lance for a long moment before answering.

"That's what I remember," she said. "We were all friends."

"Think about what I've suggested," Ryan said. "If you come up with anything to help confirm my theory, give me a call. I'm afraid the cops are looking for a body and not a killer at this point."

Beth and Ryan maneuvered back to the safety of Ryan's SUV and paused to catch their breath.

"Was that pickup in front of the management office earlier?" Ryan asked.

"I don't think so."

Jeb Jones ran from the entrance and jumped into the passenger side of the pickup. A barrel-chested man wearing a ball cap sat behind the wheel. Ryan waited before backing out and driving past the two men in the truck.

"Isn't that Johnny Stratford?" Beth asked.

"Yeah, I think so. And it looks like he's pissed off about something. He's pounding on the steering wheel hard enough to shatter it."

"That guy gave me the creeps when we talked to him the other day. He evaded most of our questions and kept staring me up and down," Beth said. "What do you suppose he's upset about?"

"Hard to tell, but I doubt if contractors are getting paid with Rigby in jail."

"Let's get back to your place," Beth said. "I've had enough for one day."

- 9.2 -

IT WAS LATE AS SLIM PULLED his sedan down the lane to J.D.'s two-story farmhouse. His headlights flashed across the cabin at the end of the tunnel-like lane. He looked closely, but didn't see any activity at the makeshift prison.

J.D. was sitting at the kitchen table when Slim walked in. He started to say something, but then noticed J.D. was on the phone. His stocky partner held up his hand, signaling to wait a minute.

Slim grabbed a Coke from the refrigerator as J.D. wrapped up the call.

"I was setting up appointments for the girls," J.D. said. "I'm havin' a little trouble with Jewell, but Shari, the little blonde, wants to get to work right away. She likes what she's seen so far."

"Are you sure she's not so strung out that she doesn't know what she wants?" Slim asked, frowning.

"She knows the deal," J.D. shot back. "She may only be seventeen, but this ain't her first rodeo."

"Have you been down to check on Campbell tonight?"

"Yeah. She's not lookin' so hot," J.D. replied. "We might not have to worry about killing her. She may croak on her own."

"I never thought it would come to this," Slim said, pulling out a chair and sitting.

"Come to what?"

"Starving her to death," Slim replied. "It's a painful way to die."

"You're not gettin' soft now, are you? This Rigby deal was your idea. I was perfectly happy with our little business we got goin' here. It was you who wanted to go for the home run."

"What if we clean her up?" Slim asked. "She's a good-lookin' woman under all that dirt and blood. She might be glad to turn a few tricks for her room and board."

"Are you nuts?" J.D. growled. "She's way too old for our clients, and we could never brainwash her like we do these teenagers. For one thing, she's not an addict. For another, she's got a home and a boyfriend to return to."

"What if I take her on as my personal project? I could drug her up, clean her up, and put some fancy clothes on her. She could be fun to have around at the end of a hard day," Slim said with a filthy grin.

"You're sicker than me," J.D. said. "It would be less risky to just kill her and toss the body in a rocky ravine."

"But it wouldn't be as much fun," Slim smirked.

"You know we'll still need to get rid of her at some point," J.D. argued. "We've been wearin' masks up 'til now. Are you gonna continue to wear masks doin' what *you're* plannin' to do?"

"Just give me a few days," Slim pleaded. "There's no hurry to kill her. The cops have all but convicted Rigby, and no one is going to look for Campbell out here."

"All right, but just a few days. Then she's gotta go."

- Day 10 -

RYAN'S CELLPHONE chirped on top of his dresser. He glanced at the bedside clock. It was 7:25.

"Who the hell could this be?" he mumbled, tossing off the bedsheet and shuffling toward the irritating noise.

"Yeah. What is it?"

"It's Detective Baker. I apologize for calling so early, but I'd like for you and Beth to meet with me this morning."

"What about? Have you found something?"

"No. There's nothing new, but Detective Phillips and the DA are convinced James Rigby is guilty of kidnapping and murder. I'm not."

"Neither am I," Ryan said. "I know the motives are there, but the personalities of Rigby and Warren just don't fit."

"Your instincts are pretty good. You were right about alerting us to Rigby. I want to get more of your thoughts. The press is too thick to meet in town. Can you meet me at Betty's Café out on 221?"

"Sure. What time?"

"An hour from now."

RYAN WAS FAMILIAR with Betty's Café. He stopped occasionally on his trips to Boone for building supplies. The diner was widely recognized for the best breakfast in the county.

Beth and Ryan entered the café at exactly 9:00. There was a waiting list for tables, but Detective Baker had arrived early. He stood at a booth near the back and waved. Wearing a sport coat and tie, he stood out among the jeans and overalls crowd.

"Thanks for coming. I didn't realize it would be this crowded," Baker said as they all slid into the booth. "Hopefully the noise will drown out our conversation."

"These folks are interested in eating, not listening to us," Ryan replied.

A waitress delivered coffee to the table with a smile. Everyone quickly agreed on cinnamon rolls. The young woman made a rehearsed pitch for the country-style breakfast as she poured coffee. After three head shakes, she departed for the rolls.

"We're glad you haven't given up on finding Sarah," Beth said. "Do you think she's still alive?"

"She's been missing nearly two weeks, but I'm not ready to turn this case into a body search just yet."

"What are you thinking at this point?" Ryan asked.

"I'm not sure, but I keep wondering how a community this size can go decades without a violent crime, and then have a murder and missing person's case in the same week."

"You think they're related?" Beth asked.

"I didn't at first, but I'm beginning to believe it's a possibility. I'm on my way to southeast Kentucky to meet the dead girl's parents. The FBI's involved now, but has agreed to let me stay on the case. We're trying to retrace Heather's steps the final weeks of her life."

"It doesn't sound like this girl and Sarah have much in common," Beth said. "She was much younger and apparently an addict."

"Where Sarah was attacked at Jefferson Peak is less than five miles from where Heather's body was found. I'm hoping if we find her killer, it will lead us to Sarah."

"How can we help?" Ryan asked.

"Detective Phillips interviewed the folks at Rolling Ridge. I've read his notes, but working the McCoy case, I'll have little time to meet with Sarah's coworkers. I was hoping you could share your impressions."

"Sure, but we're only amateur sleuths," Ryan said, "although Beth is a paralegal for a criminal law practice."

"Then you can do background checks on these people?" Baker asked.

"I guess so, unless my firm has canceled my access. I've been away nearly two weeks."

"Pull what you can find on Rigby's staff and Sarah's associates," Baker requested. "Detective Phillips is convinced he has the killer in custody, so I doubt PCPD is looking for anyone else."

"Sure, I'll look them up as soon I get back to my laptop."

"What's been your initial impression after meeting them? Anyone stand out?"

Beth looked to Ryan, nodding for him to start.

"No one strikes me as either a kidnapper or killer," Ryan began.

"Keep in mind," Baker interrupted, "most murders are committed by someone the victim knows, and motives are usually greed or passion. Could you see any of these people targeting Sarah with either motive?"

"Not really," Ryan replied. "Sarah is competitive, and I guess it's possible she and Lance Baldwin could have battled over real estate sales. But their boss, Sue Evans, claims they were a cohesive team."

"Was she ever romantically linked to any of her coworkers?" Baker asked.

"Definitely not," Beth replied. "They might have hoped for the opportunity, but I know Sarah never considered dating any of them."

"Jeb Jones thought Lance Baldwin might have dated Sarah years ago," Ryan said. "Lance went off a bit when I told him what Jones had said, insisting he and Sarah were no more than friends."

"He went off?"

"Yeah. He called Jeb a few choice names," Ryan replied.

"Other than you, when was Sarah's last serious relationship?" Baker asked.

"We don't talk about our prior relationships," Ryan replied.

"It's okay Ryan, we can discuss Fletcher," Beth said before turning to Baker. "Sarah had a nasty breakup with her college boyfriend, Guy Fletcher. Guy left Sarah to date me."

"Have either of you seen him recently?" Baker asked.

"Neither of us had seen him for years, but he showed up to help search for Sarah a couple of weeks ago."

"I thought it was strange," Ryan added. "But Beth verified Guy was on the Carolina coast at the time Sarah disappeared."

"Who vouched for his whereabouts?" Baker asked.

"Guy gave me names of people who were with him," Beth explained.

"You might want to double-check those alibis," Baker said. "The timing of his reappearance seems suspicious."

"I don't see how Fletcher fits in with blackmailing Rigby," Ryan said. "I would think Sarah's kidnapper would be someone who knew about Rigby bribing the county inspector."

"Could Fletcher have found out from Sarah?" Baker asked.

"It's possible, but I doubt it," Beth replied.

"Still, I wouldn't rule him out yet," Baker said, pushing back from the table. "I need to get on the road to Kentucky, but call my cell anytime."

He took two business cards from his wallet and tossed them on the table with a twenty.

"Enjoy your cinnamon rolls. I gotta run."

- 10.1 -

IT WAS A FOUR-HOUR DRIVE to the town of Cantrel in southeastern Kentucky, much of it over two-lane highways and county roads so remote they didn't appear on the car's GPS.

A fading billboard at the city limits boasted: *Home to the Cleanest Coal in Kentucky.* The sign had been posted years before coal-burning power plants became taboo, replaced largely by natural gas. Several nearby coal mines had closed over the past ten years, and twenty percent of the residents who hadn't fled the area were unemployed.

As Detective Baker pulled through town, it was clear the community was on the decline. Every other storefront on Main Street had a *For Lease* sign in the window.

Baker had hoped not to attract attention, but the North Carolina police plates blew his cover. His late-model Chrysler garnered stares from out-of-work men loitering on benches under the awnings of struggling stores.

The GPS directed him to turn right on Cedar Street. It appeared to be one of the finer areas of town, although that was relative. The homes, mostly single-story, were well-maintained. Lawns were mowed and several curbside mailboxes had flowers planted at the base.

After twenty years of making similar visits, Baker still dreaded meeting with grieving parents. It didn't matter what led to losing their child, such a tragedy could never be explained.

FALLEN from SIGHT

The home at 512 Cedar Street was a small, white clapboard structure. A detached two-car garage was set to the right. Baker pulled into the driveway.

A fat, yellow cat ran across the front yard and around to the side of the house as he stepped from his cruiser. Baker took a couple of slow deep breaths and then proceeded up the sidewalk to the front porch.

A redheaded woman wearing dark slacks and a white blouse opened the door before Baker could knock. Her eyes were puffy. Her thin smile was forced.

"Detective Baker?" she asked.

"Yes."

"Please come in. I'm Elaine McCoy. My husband and I've been expecting you. Jack's in the living room."

The home was spotless and decorated like a 1980s sitcom set. Baker rounded the corner of the hall, and Mr. McCoy rose from his leather recliner to greet him.

"Thanks for taking time to meet today," Baker said, extending his hand.

Jack paused, staring at the detective before accepting his handshake.

"These past two days have been gut-wrenching," Jack said. "But we want to find whoever did this to our daughter."

"We all do, sir," Baker replied.

"Please sit," Elaine said. "I'm sure it was a long drive from North Carolina. Can I get you a cold drink?"

"Thanks, but I'm fine for now," he replied, taking a small notebook from his sport coat.

"Before you begin asking us a bunch of questions that'll be painful to answer, I want you to get to know our Heather," Jack McCoy said, his voice already cracking.

"Sure. I'd like to hear about her," Baker replied, lowering his notebook to his lap.

"Here's the most recent picture we have. It was taken before a high school dance," Jack said, handing the silver-framed photo to the detective.

A petite girl wearing a long yellow dress stood before a flower-covered arch. Her red hair draped over her shoulders, and her wide smile drew you to her face.

"She was beautiful. I see the resemblance," Baker said, turning to Mrs. McCoy as he handed the photo back to Jack.

"She was a good student, captain of her soccer team, and president of her sophomore class," Jack said. "We were strict parents, but she knew we loved her."

Elaine stood and fled the room with a tissue pressed to her face.

"I don't think my wife is up to this," Jack said.

"I understand. I'll make it brief," Baker replied.

"Like I was saying, Heather was a great kid, but she seemed to change after I lost my job at the Black and Goodson Mine just over two years ago. I'd worked in the finance department for twenty years. Heather was never the same after I was laid off."

"In what way?" Baker asked.

"There's a social stigma associated with unemployed families. Kids picked on her. She worried about being able to afford college, and she got in with the wrong crowd. It seemed like there was nothing we could do. Truth be told, we actually lost her two years ago."

Recounting the past was painful. Jack bit his bottom lip and paused, but he couldn't hold back his emotions.

"Excuse me," he said, standing. "I should check on Elaine."

He returned a moment later with a glass of water, his eyes still moist.

"I'm sorry," he said. "Heather's body was returned this morning. They told us we couldn't see her, that they were unable to put her back together. Who could do such a thing to a teenage girl?"

"That's what we'd all like to know. We'll do whatever we can to find whoever's responsible."

"We've already answered questions from the FBI. What else do you want to know?"

"When did you last see or hear from Heather?"

"We haven't seen her for over a year. She called about six months ago asking for money, but we told her we'd help only if she came home. She refused."

"Do you know of anyone she might have stayed with after running away?"

"No. We checked with everyone we could think of. No one had seen her."

"Were you aware she was taking drugs?"

"Sure. Opioids are a big problem around here. One of her girlfriends got her hooked. It was downhill from there. We were advised by our doctor to put her in a rehab center. That was the last time we saw her. She ran away from the center and never came back."

"Was she ever arrested for possession, before or after she ran away?" Baker asked.

"Not before, but I heard from the father of one of her friends that a Tennessee county sheriff contacted him about three months ago. He said his daughter Tricia was arrested with another girl who fit Heather's description."

"Where in Tennessee?"

"I can't recall, but Lee Weathersby would know. He's Tricia's father. He lives about six blocks from here. Continue south down Cedar and turn right on Highpoint. His house is the third on the left."

"Has he heard from Tricia recently?" Baker asked as he jotted down the directions.

"She overdosed a couple weeks after getting bailed out of the Tennessee jail. She was found dead in a Knoxville motel," Jack replied. "She was younger than Heather--just turned seventeen when she died."

"Was there any indication Heather was with her in Knoxville?"

"No. We even had the cops check for Heather's prints and DNA."

"Is there anything else you can tell me that might help identify who's responsible for your daughter's death?" Baker asked.

"No. I've already answered every possible question, but there's something I'd like everyone to know."

"What's that?"

Mr. McCoy took a deep breath. The strain on his face was palpable.

"Heather came from a good family, an educated and hardworking family. Drugs don't care about your level of education or your W-2. Heather was a good girl, a smart girl. If this could happen to her, it could happen to anyone."

"I understand," Baker replied, returning his notebook to his coat pocket.

"Not everyone does," Jack said, rising from his chair. "Too many view us as a bunch of uneducated coal miners, so it's not a surprise when these tragedies happen to us."

"That's not the way that I think, Mr. McCoy," Baker said.

Reaching the entrance, Baker turned to shake Jack's hand. "You have my support and deepest sympathy."

BAKER SAT IN HIS CAR collecting his thoughts before backing out of the driveway. He didn't know if he was up to meeting another set of parents who'd just lost their child, but his desire for answers propelled him forward. The case had become personal to him.

The Weathersby home appeared similar to the McCoy residence. It was small and well-kept. The flag on the pole in the front yard flew at half-mast.

The sound of a barking dog inside the home greeted Baker as he stepped up the sidewalk. He stopped short of the porch. On the other side of the glass storm door was a grey and white pit-mix, clearly unhappy with the detective's appearance.

Baker waited until a tall man in jeans and dark tee shirt came to the door and grabbed the sturdy canine by the collar.

"One second," the man mouthed through the glass as he struggled to pull the dog from the entrance. He immediately returned and opened the door.

"Sorry about Butch," he said, scanning Baker from head to toe. "You're either a preacher or a cop. We've seen plenty of both the past few months."

"I'm Detective Baker with the North Carolina SBI. Are you Lee Weathersby?"

"Yeah, that's me. What's up?"

"I just came from the McCoy residence. Mr. McCoy mentioned that Heather and your daughter were friends. I was wondering if I could ask you a couple of questions."

"Her name was Tricia," he replied, stepping out onto the porch. "It'll upset my wife if you come in, but I'll talk to you here if it'll help find Heather's killer. The McCoys are good folks."

"Mr. McCoy said a Tennessee sheriff notified you several months ago that your daughter was in custody and that someone matching Heather's description was with her. Do you have the sheriff's name, or do you know the county where she was being held?"

"Yeah, I remember. It was Sheriff John Porter in Slater County. He called several times, but we were visiting friends that weekend. I called him back as soon as I picked up the voicemails, but he'd already released Tricia to someone claiming to be her cousin."

"Did he give you the name of the person providing bail?"

"It was a guy named Jarod Willard, but I can save you some time."

"How's that?"

"It was a fake ID. Jarod Willard is a dentist in Kingsport. He was nowhere near Slater County that day, or any other day as it turns out."

"Any description of the man who bailed Tricia out?" Baker asked.

"You'll need to talk to Sheriff Porter. All he or anyone at the jail could remember was the guy was wearing a ball cap and black rimmed glasses. No one could remember his hair color, or even if he had hair. Believe it or not, the jail's surveillance system didn't get a clear video of this guy."

"What about…"

"I'm sorry. You've already gone past a couple questions," Mr. Weathersby interrupted. "I've got things to do."

The dejected man turned and walked back inside.

Baker stepped from the porch and returned to his car. Still parked at the curb, he took out his cellphone and searched on Slater County, Tennessee. The Slater County seat in Richburg was 200 miles to the southwest. If he left now, it would be late when he arrived. He'd need to stay overnight in the rural Tennessee town.

Baker started his cruiser and began his return route to Boone. He'd make the trip to Slater County tomorrow.

- 10.2 -

BETH'S BACKGROUND CHECKS were yielding little information. Traffic tickets and overdue credit card payments were the most egregious offenses uncovered. She and Ryan sat at his kitchen table, poring over the notes from her searches, frustrated with the lack of progress.

"I keep coming back to one fact," Ryan said. "Whoever blackmailed Rigby knew about the soil tests and the payments to Fred Warren."

"That would include Rigby, Warren, and we assume, Sarah," Beth replied.

"And anyone those three may have told," Ryan added.

"That could be any number of people."

"Let's think about this logically," Ryan said. "Why would Rigby or Warren tell anyone? They were trying to keep their little arrangement quiet."

"Still, someone close to Rigby or Warren could have overheard their phone conversations or seen documents," Beth argued.

"Yeah. That's possible. But once learning of the bribery, why would they then kidnap Sarah?" Ryan asked.

"They wouldn't."

"Right. So it must be someone who found out from Sarah," Ryan said.

"I wonder if Sue Evans ever located Sarah's notebook," Beth said. "It wasn't in Sarah's purse, but it's something we should follow up on."

"Good idea," Ryan replied as he reached for his cellphone.

Sue was working late in her office when she received Ryan's call.

"It's Ryan Nelson. I was wondering if you ever checked with Parsons Creek PD to see if they had Sarah's notebook."

"Yeah, I called shortly after we spoke. They didn't have it."

"Did you look around the office for it?"

"A couple of times. Neither Lance nor I could find it," she replied.

"Do you think it's something James Rigby could've taken when he searched Sarah's desk?"

"It's possible, but Sarah usually kept it in her leather purse," Sue replied. "That purse was her traveling office."

"Let me know if it turns up," Ryan said.

LANCE BALDWIN WAS LOCKING his desk and getting ready to leave when he overheard Sue on the phone.

"Who was that?" he asked.

"Ryan Nelson. He was looking for Sarah's spiral notebook. I told him we never found it."

"Rigby probably took it," Lance said, continuing to clear his desk.

"Maybe," Sue replied. "But you know that Sarah usually kept it in her purse. When could he have taken it?"

"Beats me. But it all seems moot now with Rigby in jail. Beth and Ryan should just admit Sarah's gone."

"They don't strike me as people who give up easily," Sue replied.

D.R. Shoultz

- Day 11 -

THE DOOR TO THE CELLAR swung open and a pale light filled the room.

Sarah lay curled up in the opposite corner of the dank cell on the bed of pink insulation. She lifted her head slowly as her matted, soiled hair draped loose. Her drawn face was that of a street urchin, chafed and dirty. The dim light caused her to cover her sensitive eyes.

The man standing in the doorway was taller than her usual visitor and not as stout. He wore a similar stocking mask and held a large cardboard box under his left arm.

She looked to the east-facing window. Sunlight leaked through the cracks of the boards. This was not the daily exchange with her usual captor. It was too early.

"Why are you here?" Her voice was low and coarse. She raised her hand to her sore throat.

The dark silhouette at the door didn't answer.

"What do you want with me?" she strained.

The man remained silent. He bent down and placed the box on the floor just inside the doorway. He then stood and took a final look at Sarah before closing and locking the metal door.

Sarah moved like an elderly woman as she rose slowly to her knees and then to her feet. She stepped cautiously across the cell to inspect what the man had left.

The scent of warm food hit her nostrils before she reached the box. She stepped quicker and discovered a paper plate inside filled with scrambled eggs and toast.

FALLEN from SIGHT

It had been two weeks since she'd enjoyed a warm meal, surviving on scraps and crumbs since being entombed. She eagerly lifted the plate from the box and began shoveling the food into her mouth with her hand. The warm, soft eggs soothed her inflamed throat as she swallowed.

After devouring the meal, she returned to inspect the contents of the box. In addition to a half gallon of water and a large plastic bowl, she found soap, a sponge, a hairbrush, and what appeared to be first aid supplies.

Sarah squinted to read the labels on the bottles and other items, but was unable to make out what they were. She took the bottles to the boarded-up window and held them up one at a time to the slivers of light.

Aspirin, medicated lotions, creams, and bandages were among the items.

Wasting little time to make sense of the offerings, she knelt, set the bowl in front her, and filled it with water. She wet the sponge, applied soap, and wiped her forehead and cheeks. She repeated the process over and over before tending to her arms, legs, and body. The water in the bowl was a murky brown before she finished.

Sarah picked up the hairbrush and tried to pull it through her tangled locks. The process was slow and painful, but she was determined. Thirty minutes later, a pile of hair lay at her feet, and for the first time in days, her fingers were able to easily reach her tender scalp. Gritting her teeth, she rubbed antibacterial ointment on and around her head wound.

She gathered the supplies back in the box and placed the empty water bottle by the door.

Returning to her makeshift bed, she sat. Within a few minutes, her arms and legs began to weigh heavily, and her vision blurred. The pain from her head wound subsided as her drowsiness increased.

It couldn't be the aspirin.

Unable to sit, she leaned back on her elbows and stretched her legs before her. A moment later, she fell to her back onto the insulation, unconscious.

- 11.1 -

JEB JONES AND MARGE JACKSON sat in the lobby of the Rolling Ridge management office, killing time over a Diet Coke, when Marge's desk phone rang.

"Rolling Ridge. How may I help you?" she answered.

The young foreman listened closely, continuing to sip his soda.

"Yeah. I understand," Marge said.

Silence.

"Uh huh. That's good news."

Silence.

"Does that mean phase two will proceed?" Marge asked.

Jones stood and inched closer.

"Okay. I'll wait to hear back," she said, returning the phone to her desk.

"What was that about?" Jones asked.

"It was the state water and soil commission. They confirmed that about half of the land in phase two is suitable for septic systems."

"So, are we back in business?"

"Possibly. There's still the issue of how to resolve the problems in phase one. Last I heard, the Charlotte investors would need to approve a costly plan," Marge replied.

"I read this morning two of the investors have filed civil suits against Rigby, and a judge has frozen his assets, including his home," Jones said.

"I saw that, too. It's gonna be a mess for a while, but at least there's some hope of staying open," she replied.

"The subs are getting restless. They're demanding back pay for work completed," Jones said. "Johnny Stratford was giving me an earful on Tuesday. He claims to have over a hundred thousand bucks tied up in cabinets and labor."

"He's right. I've seen the invoices," Marge said.

"If we somehow get the money, I suggest we pay him first," Jones said. "That crazy bastard threatened to shoot my dog."

"You're kidding!"

"I wish I was. I once saw him throw a hammer at one of his subs. Fortunately, he missed."

"It's not looking good for Rigby," Marge said. "Did you see where they found Sarah Campbell's bloody sweater half-burned in a trash can behind his house?"

"You never know what someone's really like, do you?" Jones asked.

"I wouldn't nominate him for boss of the year, but I never in a million years saw him as a killer," Marge replied.

"It's gonna be tough to bring this place back," Jones said.

"That's for sure. I talked to Sue Evans earlier," Marge continued. "The lawyers have told her to refund earnest money to the buyers under contract. Once she's done with that, the sales office will close."

"What do you think she and Lance will do?" Jones asked.

"Probably go back to Charlotte and work for Best View Realty," Marge replied. "You and I should probably be looking for jobs, too."

"I'll be okay," Jones said. "I have options."

- 11.2 -

BEFORE HEADING BACK on the road to Richburg, Tennessee to visit the Slater County Courthouse, Detective Baker swung past the Parsons Creek Police Department. Detective Phillips was at his desk when he arrived.

"We missed you at this morning's status meeting," Phillips said.

"I got back late last night. I thought I'd stop in later and tell you what I discovered in Kentucky," Baker replied.

"Anything interesting?"

"As you'd expect, Heather McCoy's parents are torn up. They're good, hardworking people. Heather had taken off over a year ago after her father lost his job. The last time she contacted her parents was six months later," Baker said.

"No sign of her after that?" Phillips asked.

"She and a friend were arrested for possession about three months later in Slater County, Tennessee. That's where her trail goes cold."

"What about her friend? Has she shown up anywhere?"

"Yeah. Dead in a Knoxville hotel room," Baker replied. "Apparently an accidental overdose."

"So, what next?"

"I'm headed to see the sheriff in Slater County," Baker replied. "If I can find out who the sheriff released these girls to, it might lead to how Heather wound up in a creek in Jefferson Park."

"Does the sheriff have the name of the guy?" Phillips asked.

"He used a fake ID, but I'll try to piece together a description. Maybe I can find someone who saw the girls leave. It's low odds, but worth a try."

Phillips shook his head. "That's a long way to drive with so little to go on."

"You didn't see Heather's high school photo and the anguish on her parents' faces," Baker said. "It's not far at all."

He turned to leave, and took one step before Phillips stopped him.

"Say, I hear you're encouraging Ryan Nelson and the Campbell girl to continue working Sarah's case."

"They have every right to keep looking," he replied.

"We have the killer in custody and he ain't talking," Phillips said. "Those kids are just wasting their time and getting a lot of folks upset."

"As long as Sarah hasn't been found, I don't think it's a waste of their time," Baker replied. "They're convinced she's still alive."

"We'll eventually find Sarah," Phillips said.

"I guess we'll have to see who finds her first," Baker replied. "I'm hoping it's Beth and Ryan."

- 11.3 -

UNAWARE THAT BAKER had just left Parsons Creek PD, Ryan and Beth entered the front lobby looking for Detective Phillips.

"He's in," the duty officer at the front desk said. "Go on back. He's probably in his office."

Ryan knocked on Phillips' open door. The detective looked up to see the young duo in his doorway, and immediately looked back down at the work on his desk.

"Can you spare a couple minutes?" Ryan asked.

"No more than that. What's up?" Phillips grumbled.

"We haven't been hearing much about Sarah's case on TV these days," Ryan began. "We were hoping you could give us an update. Anything new?"

Uninvited, Beth and Ryan stepped inside and took a seat across from Phillips' desk. The senior detective released a disturbing exhale and leaned back.

"I'm sure that you've heard more evidence has been discovered at Rigby's home," Phillips said.

"You mean Sarah's sweater?" Beth asked.

"Yeah."

"Don't you think it's strange Rigby disposed of Sarah's sweater in a place the police were sure to check?" Ryan asked. "Is that something a murderer would normally do?"

"Have you come here for an update on the case or to challenge our investigation?" Phillips asked, leaning forward with a threatening frown.

"I'm no lawyer, but it seems you'll need more than a sweater to convict Rigby of murder," Ryan continued. "Are you getting any closer to finding Sarah?"

"That's police business," Phillips shot back. "Now if you don't mind, I need to get back to work."

"We're also here looking for something that belonged to Sarah," Ryan said. "We haven't been able to locate the spiral notebook she kept in her purse."

"I told Sue Evans we didn't have it," Phillips complained.

"That was several days ago. We thought it might have turned up by now, maybe at Rigby's home."

"No. We haven't seen it. What's so important about this notebook?" Phillips asked.

"Sarah used it as her work diary," Beth replied. "We're curious what may have been entered the days before she disappeared."

"It would be a good source of information," Phillips agreed. "If you find the notebook, we'd like to take a look at it."

"And you'll let us know if it turns up?" Ryan asked.

"I guess so."

FALLEN from SIGHT

- 11.4 -

SLATER COUNTY CORRECTIONS was located one block north of the 150-year-old Richburg, Tennessee courthouse. The one-story stone building was fortified with black iron bars covering the small windows and entry door.

It was afternoon when Detective Baker entered the modest lobby of the jailhouse and found the front desk unoccupied. As he waited, he studied the room.

The metal door leading to the jail cells was slightly ajar, hopefully indicating there were no prisoners. Fifty years of scuff marks from the heels of criminals being dragged back to the cells marked a trail across the tile floor. Vinyl chairs separated by low tables stacked with dog-eared magazines lined the far wall, giving the room a 1950s barbershop feel.

Baker looked to the corners of the room at the ceiling where surveillance cameras would likely be affixed. There were none.

"Anyone here? I'm looking for Sheriff Porter!" he called.

A spindly, middle-aged deputy appeared from a back office dressed in a khaki uniform. If Barney Fife had an older brother, this could have been him. *Deputy Glen Gentry* was displayed on his name tag.

"I'm Detective Baker. I called and left a message about needing to speak with Sheriff Porter. Is he around today?"

"Nope," the deputy replied.

"Do you know where he is?"

"Yep."

Baker frowned, becoming irritated with the one-word answers.

"Where is he?"

"He's out on the edge of town in Vista View Gardens. He had a heart attack a week ago--his third and his last."

"He's dead? Why didn't someone return my call and tell me?" Baker asked, his frown now a glare.

"I guess I forgot to check his voicemail. I haven't had time to change his recording."

"Who's the acting sheriff?"

"You're lookin' at him. How can I help you?" Gentry asked.

Baker rolled his eyes and took a deep breath.

"About three months ago, two girls were arrested for drug possession and held here," Baker began. "Their names were Heather McCoy and Tricia Weathersby. Do you recall them?"

"Yeah, I do. One of them OD'd shortly after that if I remember right."

"That's correct. Tricia was found dead in a Knoxville hotel. I'm working the Heather McCoy case. Her body was found in a state park in North Carolina a couple of weeks ago. She'd been murdered."

"This is all terrible news, but what does this have to do with you coming here?"

"You released the two girls to a man claiming to be Jarod Willard. I'm trying to find him to see where they might have gone after that."

"We've plowed this ground before," the deputy said. "I'm not sure you're gonna come up with anything new."

"Bear with me," Baker said. "Who saw the guy posting bail for the girls?"

FALLEN from SIGHT

"It was just me and Sheriff Porter. First shift had ended and I agreed to stick around for a few more hours."

"What did the guy look like?"

"It's all in the Tennessee SBI report. Don't you SBI guys talk with each other?"

"Please, just humor me, Deputy."

Gentry frowned in disgust.

"The guy wore glasses and had a ball cap pulled down over his forehead. He claimed he was next of kin. We tried calling the parents of the Weathersby girl, but no one answered."

"Can you tell me anything else about him? Height, weight, clothes?"

"He was about my height, maybe six feet with an average or slight build. I think he was wearing jeans and a light-colored jacket. I can go get my statement to the SBI."

"I assume he provided an ID?" Baker asked.

"Sure. That's required to release anyone."

"Did he look like his photo?" Baker asked mockingly.

"As far as I remember, but those ID photos are small, and my eyes aren't what they used to be," Gentry admitted.

"Could I get a copy?"

"Yeah, but you know the name and address are false."

"I'm aware, but the guy must think he looks like the photo or he wouldn't be using it."

"Give me a minute," Gentry said. "I'll go pull the file."

The deputy returned a couple of minutes later from the back office with a manila folder. *T. Weathersby* was scribbled on the tab.

"Here's a copy of the ID," Gentry said, turning the file toward Baker.

Baker picked up the ID and took a closer look. Jarrod Willard was a generic looking, young white male, 31 years old, with short dark hair and blue eyes.

"The guy in this photo has a small mole on his left cheek. Did the man who bailed out these girls have a mole?"

"Gee, I don't recall," Gentry replied, unfazed by his oversight.

"Seems like something you might've checked before turning over two teenage girls to him," Baker scoffed. "Can I keep this?"

"Sure. It's a copy."

Baker stuffed the photo into his coat pocket and turned to leave.

Stepping outside, he noticed *Casper's Caffeine Emporium* across the street. Two cars were parked out front and a neon *Open* sign flickered in the front window. Baker waited for a red pickup to pass and then approached the quaint storefront.

Two booths against the far wall were occupied by workmen enjoying a late lunch. Four red-topped stools lined the short café bar. A man in slacks and a dress shirt sat reading a newspaper atop the far stool. Baker slid onto the near seat.

"What can I get you, honey?" asked a plump waitress wearing a hairnet and a friendly smile.

"A black coffee and one of those sweet rolls," Baker said, pointing to a display of decadence behind the counter.

The waitress returned with the coffee and roll.

"Anything else?" she asked.

"No thanks. This is fine."

"You're not from these parts, are you?"

"No. I'm just here for the day on business."

"Not much business goes on around here," she chuckled. "What kinda business you in?"

"I'm a North Carolina police detective."

"Whoa. That's a different story. Should be plenty of business for a detective," she replied.

"How long have you worked here?"

"Pretty much since it opened. This is Pop's place," she replied.

Baker turned and looked across the street at the county corrections building.

"You have a pretty good view of what goes on across the street," he said.

"Yeah. It's not all that interesting, though--mainly drunks and druggies going in and coming out."

"I'm looking for a man who bailed out two young girls about three months ago."

"What did the guy do?" she asked.

"Maybe nothing, but both of the girls are dead now."

She gasped, clutching her chest.

Baker handed the fake ID to the waitress.

"You wouldn't happen to remember seeing this man with two young girls? He bailed them out around seven on a Saturday night."

"I can't say I recognize this guy," she said, studying the photo, "but I do remember seeing a fella leave the jail with two girls a few months ago. A customer at the counter saw them first. He made a crude comment. Something like 'I bet that guy's gonna have fun tonight.'"

"Did you get a good look at him?"

"Not really. It was getting dark. I could see the girls were young and dressed like tramps," she replied. "But I didn't pay much attention to him."

"Did you notice the car he was driving?"

"Just that it was a dark sedan, blue or black I think, and it might have been foreign. I remember it looked out of place in Richburg."

"What about the plates? Were they Tennessee plates?"

"Honey, I'm a waitress, not Scully from *The X-Files*," she teased.

"Do you remember anything else? Anything at all?" Baker prodded.

"Not really," she replied. "The girls got in the back seat and he drove off. That's it."

"Did you tell any of this to the police?"

"I haven't talked to the cops about this," she replied. "Pop said detectives from Knoxville came asking if we had security cameras. They went on their way after he told them we didn't."

Baker took a couple quick sips of coffee, wrapped his sweet roll in a napkin, and stood to leave.

"Thanks for your time. You've been a great help."

FALLEN from SIGHT

- 11.5 -

THE CELLAR WAS AS DARK as a moonless night when Sarah's eyes cracked open. She lay motionless atop her makeshift bed, her memory clouded.

Had daylight come and gone?

It took several minutes for her eyes to adjust to the darkness and to muster enough energy to push herself to her knees. Her throat was dry and burning, and her head throbbed like a bad hangover. She reached around, looking for her water bottle.

Sarah bumped against the cardboard box, which triggered thoughts of the tall visitor. Her foggy mind slowly cleared, and she recalled her captor coming with food and supplies. She remembered washing her face and arms.

Sarah reached to her hair. It almost felt normal.

The eggs!

She lowered her face toward the box, looking for more food, but she'd eaten it all.

Sarah had no way of knowing how long she'd slept. She didn't even remember if the regular nightly exchange had occurred.

Maybe I missed it.

She found the water bottle and sat on the bed with her back against the wall, staring into the darkness.

Minutes later the sound of footsteps and the high-pitched whining of a girl came from the other side of the door. Sarah sat erect and pulled the box of supplies closer to her.

Keys rattled against the padlock and the door burst open. The silhouette of the stocky masked captor stood in the doorway, clenching the arm of a slender woman.

"Get your head straight, and I might let you come back to work!" the man shouted.

"No!" the girl shrieked, before being thrust into the dark cellar. She fell to her knees but quickly got to her feet and ran back toward the doorway. The captor stepped back, and the door slammed in her face.

The young girl turned away from the door and her eyes darted around the room, unable to see anything.

"Your eyes will adjust," Sarah said softly.

The girl stiffened and clutched her chest.

"Who are you?" she asked.

"Sarah. Sarah Campbell. Who are you?"

"Jewell Anders. What is this place?"

"I wish I knew," Sarah replied. "I've been down here nearly two weeks as best I can tell. I was out hiking, was hit on the head, and woke up here."

"Do you work for them?" Jewell asked.

"Work for who?"

"J.D. and Slim. You know. Us girls do what they want and they give us what we need."

"I don't know," Sarah said, shocked by what the girl just told her. "What do these men look like? Have you seen them without their masks?"

"They don't wear masks. I don't know why J.D. put one on just to throw me in here."

"Describe them," Sarah insisted.

"J.D. is about my dad's age, late forties I'd guess. He's stocky with short dark hair. It has some grey," Jewell began. "Slim's younger, taller and nicer. Kinda cute."

"How do you know them?" Sarah asked.

"Slim bailed me outta jail up in Tennessee. It's where I'm from. I was hurtin' bad, and no one else seemed to care."

"Do you know where we are? Is there a town nearby?"

"I'm not real good with directions. I know we're in North Carolina. J.D. drives us girls to Charlotte from here. It takes a couple of hours."

"What's in Charlotte?"

"That's where the money is, J.D. says. Most of the men are okay, but I told J.D. I wouldn't go back to see Jackson. He's too rough."

"Is that why he threw you in here?"

"Yeah. He said if I wanted to keep gettin' the good stuff, *he'd* decide who I was with."

Sarah paused, her mind racing.

"I have a bottle of water. Are you thirsty?"

Jewell hesitated before reaching out with one arm to feel her way.

"Where are you?" Jewell asked.

"Follow my voice," Sarah said in a comforting tone.

Jewell stepped slowly across the floor until she touched Sarah's shoulder. Sarah reached up and took her hand.

"Please sit," Sarah said. "I've made a soft place here in the corner."

"How've you survived two weeks in this place?" Jewell asked as she sat.

"They bring me scraps of food, water, and a bucket for waste," Sarah replied.

"Oh my God! You poop in a bucket?"

"You do what you have to do to survive," Sarah said. "That's what we're doing now—surviving."

Jewell's eyes began to water. She reached to wipe her running nose. "I want outta here," she cried.

Her voice was that of a young, vulnerable girl. Sarah reached to put her arm around the teenager.

"We'll get through this," Sarah said.

"ARE YOU NUTS? You tossed Jewell in with Sarah Campbell?" Slim screamed. "They're bound to exchange information!"

"What's the big deal?" J.D. argued. "We knew we'd have to get rid of the Campbell girl sooner or later, and the only people Jewell ever sees are sex-crazed men. She could tell them anything and they wouldn't believe her, or even listen to her for that matter."

"I don't know about this," Slim replied. "You're taking a lot of risk with my life."

J.D. walked to the kitchen and slid open a drawer. Reaching inside, he pulled out a .45 caliber handgun.

"If you're that worried about your damn future," J.D. spit through tight lips, "then take this down to the cellar and put a slug in each of their pretty heads. I already have a place in mind to ditch their bodies."

"You'd like that, wouldn't you?" Slim snapped back. "You'd like for me to do your dirty work--for me to have the blood on *my* hands."

"I keep reminding you that we'd be sittin' pretty, running a profitable little business, if you hadn't brought Sarah Campbell into the mix," J.D. argued.

"It doesn't mean we need to add murder to our résumés," Slim countered. "Until now, Campbell had no idea who kidnapped her. We could've cut her loose in the woods, and no one would've known."

"She'd eventually figure it out," J.D. said, pointing the gun toward the cabin. "Dead girls don't talk, Slim. You'll rest easier as soon as you accept that."

J.D.'s cellphone chirped and he snatched it from his back pocket. A knot formed in his throat, seeing Deputy Gentry's caller ID.

"What's up?" J.D. asked.

"A detective from your parts was here today. Detective Baker from the SBI. Do you know him?"

"I know the name. What did he want?" J.D. asked.

"He was asking questions about your boy."

"What kinda questions?"

"He wanted a description of who bailed out the dead girls. He asked if the guy looked like the ID he was using."

"What did you tell him?" J.D. asked.

"Nothing that isn't already known. I said he wore a cap that made it hard to describe him."

"Anything else?"

"He asked if your boy had a mole on his cheek like the one in the photo. I said I couldn't remember."

"Do you think he bought it?"

"This cop seemed more determined than those from a couple months ago. You better be on the lookout."

"Let me know if he comes back," J.D. said before slipping his phone back into his pocket.

J.D. turned to Slim, his face as serious as a heart attack.

"What was that all about?" Slim asked.

"We have a problem."

- Day 12 -

IT WAS EARLY MORNING when Baker spun the photo ID across Detective Phillips' desk.

"I'm betting this guy is trafficking girls across state lines," Baker announced.

Phillips pried the photo off his desktop and studied it.

"Doctor Jarod Willard? This is your guy?" he asked.

"No, but someone who looks like him is," Baker replied. "He's probably preyed on other girls. We should get this photo out to county corrections facilities across eastern Kentucky and Tennessee."

"Why that area?"

"First of all, he's already struck there. Second, poverty, drugs, and a desire for a better life are all present in the region. It's a perfect formula for producing the girls he targets."

"We can't put this photo out. This Willard guy would sue our asses off," Phillips said.

"We can construct a composite sketch to match the photo," Baker suggested. "The SBI in Charlotte has software that can produce an identical sketch in a few minutes. Get the photo to them, and they'll turn it around this morning."

"If this guy brought the McCoy girl back here, we should get the sketch to the local press, too," Phillips said.

"If you do, you'd better be prepared for a shitload of calls," Baker warned. "This guy's features are pretty common. Six feet tall, dark-haired men in their early thirties are not unique."

"So, what are you suggesting? We just send it to the county jails?"

"That would be my recommendation, at least until we get a better description of the kidnapper and his car," Baker replied. "Then we can get it to local police departments as well."

"Consider it done."

Baker stepped from the office as Sgt. Williams entered, neither acknowledging the other.

"What was that about?" the stocky lawman asked.

"Baker thinks this guy is connected to the Heather McCoy murder. Someone looking like this fella bailed her out of a Tennessee county jail."

Williams picked up the ID with his stubby fingers, looked at it for a brief moment, and tossed it back to the table.

"Look like anyone you know?" Phillips asked.

"Yeah. I know half a dozen guys who look like this," he smirked. "Take the uniform off of Jeff Bronson, and it could be him."

Phillips looked at the ID again.

"You're right. There *is* a resemblance. I guess Baker has a point. It would be a mistake to release this to the public."

"I'm not sure what good this photo will do, other than rule out short blonde men," Williams scoffed.

"Still, get copies of the SBI sketch to the patrol units," Phillips ordered. "We're expanding the door-to-door search radius today. It's one more thing they can ask about."

"If you say so," Williams replied.

- 12.1 -

SARAH WOKE TO SUNLIGHT seeping through the cracks in the boards over the east-facing window. Still asleep, the slender frame of Jewell Anders lay next to her. Long satiny hair covered the teenager's face.

The toilet pail remained in the far corner of the room, signifying the nightly exchange never occurred. All the food was gone, and the cellar smelled like an outhouse.

Before falling asleep, Sarah used the remaining water to treat her head wound and wash down two aspirin.

It had been over twenty-four hours since Sarah had eaten. Her stomach rumbled in pain, and now, even if food came, there were two mouths to feed.

Heavy footsteps descended the stairway, growing louder as they approached the cellar door. Sarah tensed, her movement stirring Jewell. The teen flinched and sat up as the door flung open.

The stocky kidnapper stood in the doorway, his face covered by a stocking, holding a large iron pan and a water bottle.

"Enjoy this. It could be your last," he growled, sliding the pan onto the cement floor and tossing the plastic bottle toward the two young women.

Sarah reached for the projectile, but it sped past her hands, striking her in the chest with a dull thud. The container tumbled to her feet. She struggled to find the bottle in the dim light as its life-supporting contents flowed onto the makeshift bed. Only half of the precious liquid remained by the time she lifted it from the floor.

Their captor grinned at their plight before turning and slamming the door behind him.

Jewell sat motionless, eyes wide, petrified with fear, as Sarah hurried to retrieve the skillet. She returned to the soggy bed and sat next to the frightened teen.

"It's scrambled eggs," Sarah said. "Here's a spoon I found in this box. You go first."

"Are you sure? You must be starving," Jewell said, accepting the utensil.

"Go ahead," Sarah insisted.

Jewell took the pan and placed it on her lap. Squinting in the darkness, she used the spoon to push half the contents to one side, saving the other half for Sarah.

It took little time for them to devour their portions. After a couple of swigs of water, Sarah set the bottle into the cardboard box.

Sarah looked toward the toilet pail in the far corner. Her captor hadn't exchanged it. She needed to go, but the room already smelled like a house full of feral cats.

"Would you mind?" she asked Jewell. "I'm sorry, but I really need to use the pail."

Jewell turned toward the wall as Sarah stepped across the room to relieve herself. Sarah returned and tore a flap off the cardboard box, using it to cover the pail.

"There. That might help," she said, sitting next to Jewell.

"They laced the food with something," Jewell said calmly.

"What do you mean?" Sarah asked, surprised by her comment.

"I can feel it. I was coming down, but I'm fine now," she replied. "Don't you feel lightheaded?"

Sarah was slow to respond. She lifted her arms and then gradually lowered them to her side.

"I'm dizzy," Sarah replied.

"It's probably China White," Jewell said. "It's more potent than morphine. J.D. has plenty in the house. I think he sells it."

"China White?"

"Yeah, street fentanyl. Just the slightest amount and you'll float like a cloud. A little bit more or a bad dose, and you'll be dead in minutes."

"Dead? Do you think he's trying to kill us?" Sarah asked.

"We wouldn't be talking now if he wanted to kill us," Jewell replied. "He's just controlling us, to keep us quiet."

Sarah fell back onto her elbows, her eyes rolling back in her head. "What's happening?" she groaned.

"Your tolerance is lower than mine. You're gonna sleep for a while."

Jewell reached to Sarah and caught her as she slumped into her arms. She lowered her sluggish cellmate onto the bed.

For several minutes, Jewell listened closely to Sarah's rhythmical breathing, making sure she was just sleeping.

Jewell grasped Sarah's hand and leaned against the wall. She closed her eyes, waiting for the drug to once again dull the pain in her life.

- 12.2 -

THE SKETCH OF THE MAN suspected of bailing out Heather McCoy had been distributed to sheriffs and correctional institutions across southeastern Kentucky and eastern Tennessee. Patrol officers in cities and counties neighboring Parsons Creek also had the image downloaded to their vehicles' onboard computers for easy viewing.

It was approaching sunset when a knock came to the front door of the farmhouse. J.D. rose from watching TV and hurried to the kitchen. He retrieved the loaded .45 and slipped it into his belt behind him, covering it with his untucked shirt.

He returned to find two uniformed officers standing on the front porch.

"This is a first. I can't recall getting a visit from Parsons Creek PD before. How can I help you guys?" J.D asked.

"I'm Officer Bronson and this is Officer Smitgall. Is this your farm?"

"Yeah. I have about twenty acres out here."

"We're looking for anyone who may have seen this girl or man in the area," Officer Bronson said, handing J.D. the photos of Heather McCoy and the sketch of her alleged kidnapper.

J.D. quickly glanced at the photos and passed them back.

"I haven't seen either one of them. But the guy could be you."

"I'm getting a lot of that," Bronson replied, shaking his head.

Muffled calls came floating down the lane toward the house. J.D. jerked his head in the direction of the cabin.

"What was that?" Bronson asked.

"Probably my calves," J.D. replied. "They get hungry this time of day. If you don't mind, I should get down there."

The officers paused to listen, but the calls had stopped.

"If you see anyone suspicious, give us a shout," Bronson said as they turned to leave.

J.D. watched as the two officers returned to their cruiser and pulled down the lane toward the county road.

He went back to the kitchen and slid open the drawer where the gun had been. He retrieved a four-inch-long silencer from the back, screwed it onto the muzzle of the .45, and replaced the gun inside.

J.D.'s phone rang atop the kitchen table.

"What is it?" the sex trafficker growled into the phone.

"Thought you should know a rendering of your boy has been sent to county jails across Tennessee. I just got mine," Deputy Gentry said.

"The cops are going door-to-door with the photo. They were just here. It's not a very good likeness of Slim, but I can't take any chances," J.D. said, pacing the kitchen.

"One of the other county sheriffs is bound to recognize him. Maybe you should cut them in," Gentry suggested.

"I didn't want to pay your greedy ass, but I had no choice!" J.D. shouted. "Besides, who's to say these deputy dawgs would cooperate."

"What are you gonna do?" Gentry asked.

"It's time to cut off some of the loose ends," he replied, staring at the .45 in the kitchen drawer. "And let this be a lesson to you."

"What do you mean?"

"You'd better keep your mouth shut because you're a loose end, too."

- 12.3 -

RUMORS WERE SENDING the residents of Parsons Creek into a frenzy after the sketch of the suspected kidnapper was leaked to the press. It was being reported that Heather McCoy's killer had been spotted in the area, and the door-to-door searches were an attempt to flush him out.

Chief Adkins held an unscheduled news conference at city hall in an attempt to calm the town.

"The door-to-door search for clues was underway before we received the photo of the suspect," Adkins began. "Around-the-clock patrol of our streets is ongoing. The citizens of Parsons Creek are as safe as any town in the state."

He had barely finished his opening comments when a dozen hands shot into the air and the rumble of the crowd drowned him out.

"What about the Campbell girl? Have you found her body?"

"Is it true a sex trafficking ring is operating in this county?"

"What's holding up progress in these cases?"

"Why hasn't the FBI taken over? Isn't this in their jurisdiction now?"

It took Adkins thirty minutes to get off the stage and back to the solitude of his office.

"FIREARM SALES AS FAR AWAY as Boone have gone wild," Beth said, repeating what she'd just heard on a nightly cable news channel. "Do you have a gun in the house?"

"I have a .38 in the glovebox of my Bronco and a rifle in my bedroom closet," Ryan replied. "I take them to the range every so often, but I don't know if I could aim at anything living, not even a squirrel."

"A fine protector you'd be," Beth quipped.

"I've always hoped my NRA stickers on the front door would keep bad guys away. You know, like the people who plant security systems signs in front of their shrubs," Ryan said. "Besides, Patches would bark his head off if anyone so much as stepped into the yard."

"Do you think this guy's really out there?" she asked.

"Hard to tell. Detective Baker said he thinks the guy's running girls out of eastern Tennessee. Why he'd bring them to Parsons Creek is the question. It seems Charlotte would be a better headquarters."

"There's no way Sarah would fall victim to a sex trafficker," Beth said. "I can't believe Baker still thinks there's a connection."

"I admit it's not that obvious to me either, other than evil has no boundaries."

"For them to be connected, Sarah would have had to share knowledge of the bribery scandal with someone connected to sex trafficking," Beth summarized. "Who on earth could that be?"

"Maybe Phillips is right in believing Rigby *is* the killer and the blackmailer was Warren."

"I won't accept that. It would mean Sarah is gone forever," Beth said, her voice cracking.

Ryan approached to comfort her.

"Let's focus on Sarah's missing notebook," he said. "It'll take our minds off this at-large kidnapper."

"The notebook must've fallen out of her purse and is lost," Beth said. "Where else could it be? It's not in her house. It's not in her desk. It wasn't found at Rigby's home. No one in her office has seen it."

"I'd bet someone she works with has it," Ryan said.

"We've spoken to everyone. They all seem to be telling the truth," Beth argued.

"I'm still wondering why Sarah asked Lance if he thought Jeb Jones was trustworthy. She must have been considering telling him something," Ryan said.

"And he does resemble the sketch I saw on TV tonight," Beth added. "Maybe we should ask Phillips to pay him another visit."

"I don't think Phillips' heart's in it," Ryan said. "He's ready to close the case on Sarah's disappearance. I think it's time to take the bull by the horns--or Jeb Jones by the neck."

- 12.4 -

SLIM TURNED OUT the lights and retired to the bedroom of his modest ranch home on the edge of Parsons Creek. While brushing his teeth, he heard a door creak toward the front of the house. Heart racing, he crept silently down the hall.

As he stepped into the kitchen and flipped on the light, a man appeared in his peripheral vision from behind the wall. He snapped his head to the left, but before Slim could get a clear look, a rope looped around his neck and drew tight.

With his last breath trapped in his lungs, Slim frantically reached for the rope with both hands as his eyes bulged. The powerful arms of his assailant made it pointless to fight. Slim's arms flayed and his legs kicked violently during his last moments of life, but his suffering was brief. He died not knowing it was his partner who squeezed the life from his body.

J.D. dropped Slim's limp body to the floor. With gloved hands, he lifted the warm corpse to his shoulder and carried it to the garage.

He took a ten-foot length of the same rope used to kill Slim, stood on a chair, and looped it over the rail of the garage door. J.D. then tied one end of the rope around Slim's neck and hoisted him off the ground. Next, he tied the other end of the rope tight to the rail with Slim's feet dangling a few feet from the floor. He then kicked the chair over and positioned it below the feet of his dead partner.

J.D. returned to the kitchen and removed a typewritten note from his pocket, placing it on the table. He then walked through the house and erased any signs that Slim planned to live another day.

Slim's toothbrush was replaced in its holder and the sink rinsed. The book on his nightstand was closed and placed in a drawer. All the lights inside the house were turned off. Only the light in the garage was on when J.D. slinked out the back door and disappeared down the alley to his waiting pickup.

- Day 13 -

MARGE JACKSON'S RED TOYOTA was the lone vehicle in the Rolling Ridge parking lot when Beth and Ryan pulled beside it.

They entered the lobby of the management office to find a pile of folders on Marge's desk. With a cigarette dangling from her lips like a fishhook in a carp's mouth, she was sorting through the files and pulling documents to be shredded.

"Doing a little housecleaning?" Ryan asked.

"It's not what it looks like," she replied. "The auditors and SBI have already combed through these files. I'm just takin' out the personal and irrelevant stuff so whoever takes over this place won't need to do it."

"Rolling Ridge is closing down?" Beth asked.

"It sure looks that way. The investors can't come to an agreement on financing, and the cost to get phase one up to code is still undefined. It's a real mess."

"What will happen with all the employees and contractors?" Ryan asked.

"The last paychecks have gone out. I'm here today on my own time. I just don't have anything else to do."

"Do you expect Jeb Jones to be in today?" Beth asked. "We'd like to talk with him."

"I haven't heard from him this morning. Jeb usually calls me on his way into the office. He used to do it to get an early warning of Mr. Rigby's mood. I guess those days are over."

"We'll go ahead and drive over to his place," Ryan said.

"Sorry you have to make that trip, but I doubt Jeb'll be coming around here much anymore."

TRAFFIC WAS LIGHT on their drive. Red maple leaves and yellow birch foliage were already blowing in waves across the county road, indicating winter was just around the corner. The hillsides were a montage of autumn colors.

"Sarah loves this time of year," Beth said. "I hope she gets a chance to enjoy this."

"It's one of the most beautiful places on earth," Ryan replied. "If evil can surface here, then there's no place to escape it."

Jeb's black F-150 was parked beside the cabin in front of the garage. His brown and white coonhound came running and howling as Ryan pulled his Bronco to the front of the single-story home.

"I hope he remembers us," Beth said.

"You'll be fine," Ryan replied. "Coonhounds slobber and howl, but rarely bite."

"Rarely?"

"Yeah. And usually they target city folks."

Beth shot Ryan a that's-not-funny stare and stepped out of the SUV. The inquisitive coonhound followed them to the front porch, with Ryan staying between Beth and the dog.

Ryan pounded three times on the heavy oak door. After waiting a long moment with no response, he knocked again.

"He must be here somewhere," Beth said. "His pickup is right there."

"The dog came from behind the house. Maybe Jeb's back there," Ryan suggested.

They stepped from the porch and walked to the backyard, but Jeb was not in the area. The coonhound loped toward the garage and pawed at the door.

"He must be in there," Ryan said. "Let's see if the door is locked."

Ryan looked through the four-panel window before testing the lock. The light was on in the garage. Large cabinets were stacked down the center, but he couldn't see Jeb. He turned the doorknob and the door opened.

"Anyone home?" Ryan called out.

Jeb stepped from around the stacked cabinets wearing a dust mask.

"Sorry, I didn't hear you. I've been sanding cabinet doors," he said, pulling the mask from his face. "What's up?"

"It's something Lance Baldwin told us. He said Sarah once asked him if he trusted you. To me, that sounds like she was about to confide in you about something. Did she share any secrets with you?"

"What? You drove all the way out here to ask me *that*?"

"Let me be more specific," Ryan said, stepping closer to Jones. "Did she tell you Rigby bribed the county inspector?"

"No! Of course not. We rarely spoke about anything other than business. She was all about getting her closings done on time."

"Were you aware of the bribes?" Ryan asked.

"No, but I'm not surprised. Rigby had a habit of stepping over the line."

"In what way?" Beth asked.

"I knew much of the land in phase one would never perc, and I suspected he rigged the tests. He also would occasionally tell me to substitute lower quality building materials to cut costs."

"So, you knew you were working for a crook?"

"Listen! I just did what I was told. I played no role in the fake soil reports or the bribery, and no one ever died because their knockoff bathroom fixtures came from China instead of Kohler, Wisconsin."

"What can you tell me about Sarah's notebook—the one she kept in her purse?" Ryan asked.

"What about it? I knew she kept notes, but I don't see how that affects me."

"Do you have the notebook, or do you know where it is?" Ryan pressed.

"You two are starting to get under my skin. Now get out of my garage before I take this sander to your faces!"

Ryan snapped. He stepped forward, grabbed Jeb by his shirt collar, and pushed him into the stack of cabinets, toppling them over.

Jeb jumped back to his feet and took a roundhouse swing at Ryan. He jerked his head back and Jeb's swing flew past. The momentum of the missed punch caused the foreman to stumble. Ryan stepped forward and grabbed Jeb's other arm, pinning it behind him. He then drove Jeb face-first into the garage wall and held him there.

"You better be telling us the truth," Ryan warned through his clenched jaw. "If not, I'll be back, and I'll stuff your beaten body into one of these cabinets."

Ryan pulled Jeb away from the wall and tossed him to the floor.

"I'm gonna have you arrested for assault!" Jeb shouted as Ryan and Beth stepped out the back door and hurried to his SUV.

"I take it you didn't believe him," Beth said, hiding a smirk.

"I've never liked that guy," Ryan snarled. "He deserved that, if for nothing else, for doing Rigby's dirty work."

"Just remember, you're not going to be much help finding Sarah if you're in jail."

Ryan pulled back onto the county highway and headed toward Parsons Creek. As they neared town, three police cars with sirens blaring and lights flashing shot past in the opposite direction.

"Could it be Sarah?" Beth gasped.

Ryan pulled off the road and whipped the bulky Bronco around, sending a rooster tail of gravel into the air as he sped toward the strobing police lights.

Three miles later, the police cars slid to a stop in the front yard of a ranch home on the edge of town. Detective Phillips, Sgt. Williams, and Officers Bronson and Smitgall were among those responding.

Beth and Ryan pulled to the far side of the road and parked. The lawmen jumped from their vehicles, scurried to the garage, and forced the side door open.

"Do you know whose house this is?" Beth asked.

"I have no idea."

Detective Phillips was the first to reach the body dangling from the garage door rails. He pulled on latex gloves before testing the exposed arm of the corpse.

"Stiff as a board. Get the coroner out here, ASAP!" Phillips instructed. "Smitgall, tape off the area. Everybody else, glove up and wait for forensics to arrive."

Beth and Ryan watched as yellow tape was stretched around the perimeter of the house.

"I can't take this. I have to find out what's going on," Beth said, jumping from the SUV. Ryan followed as she jogged across the street toward the house. Officer Smitgall met them before they reached the tape.

"You need to get back to your vehicle," he said. "This is a crime scene."

"I'm Sarah Campbell's sister. Is Sarah in there?" Beth pleaded.

"I'm sorry, but I can't answer any questions at this time. Check back at PCPD later."

"Come on, Beth," Ryan said. "Let's go wait at the police station. Detective Baker will let us know as soon as he can."

Reluctantly, Beth turned and walked with Ryan to his vehicle.

"Can you jot down the address on the mailbox?" Ryan asked.

"I'll do better than that," she replied. It took a minute to find the county register of deeds website on her phone and type the address into the search field.

Beth's mouth fell slack and the color drained from her face.

"I don't believe it," she muttered.

"What is it?"

"This is Lance Baldwin's house."

- 13.1 -

IT TOOK 90 MINUTES for SBI Forensics to arrive from Greensboro. By then, Phillips and his team were pacing the garage, wondering what awaited them inside the house.

Sean McGinn, a stubby, middle-aged man with a creative comb-over, headed the forensics team. Gloved and with feet bagged, he was the first to enter the house. His team of investigators followed with cameras and sterile plastic bags for gathering evidence.

"It looks like this place has been scrubbed," Phillips said as he entered. "No bachelor lives like this."

The house looked like a *Better Homes & Gardens* magazine spread. Everything was in its place. Counters, tables, and floors were cleared and clean. Even the throw pillows were plumped and propped against the arms of the sofa.

"Who reported the death?" McGinn asked.

"A kid came to borrow a mower and saw the body hanging in the garage through the side door window," Phillips replied.

"Anyone question him?"

"Yeah. We got a statement, but he didn't know much else. He didn't see anyone come or go."

"On the table!" a younger member of McGinn's team exclaimed. "It's a note."

"Get a photo before you move it," McGinn ordered.

After taking photos of the tabletop and note, Phillips picked up the folded sheet of paper and laid it flat.

"Looks like a suicide note," Phillips announced.

He read it aloud:

I thought I'd save the taxpayers of Birch County the time and expense of a trial. With my sketch on cable news, I knew it was a matter of time before I'd be behind bars.

I never wanted to see any of the girls killed, and I am truly sorry for the grief I've caused their families, especially Heather McCoy's parents. I go to my death accepting sole responsibility for the carnage I left behind. May God forgive me.

-- Lance Baldwin

"Anybody know anything about this guy?" McGinn asked.

"I interviewed him after Sarah Campbell disappeared," Phillips replied. "He and Sarah worked together selling retirement homes out at Rolling Ridge."

"You didn't suspect anything then?"

"Not really. Seemed like a responsible, hardworking young man. I guess I couldn't have been more wrong."

"Something's amiss here," McGinn said. "This guy admits to kidnapping the McCoy girl and playing a role in her death, but fails to offer anything about Sarah Campbell."

"Sorry I'm late. I was on my way to Tennessee to check out another teen arrest and release," Detective Baker announced as he stepped into the kitchen. "What have I missed?"

"The man hanging in the garage like a Thanksgiving turkey is Lance Baldwin, a coworker of Sarah Campbell's," Phillips replied. "His suicide note confesses to the Heather McCoy murder and implies he's trafficking girls, but makes no mention of Sarah Campbell. There. Now you're up to speed."

"If he's trafficking girls, I doubt he's working alone," Baker said. "Especially if he was holding down a day job. He might have time to pick them up, but he's probably passing them off to someone else, or to a network of traffickers."

"Hear that, people?" McGinn called to his team. "Turn this place upside down. We're looking for anything pointing to this guy's partners."

Baker took a close look at the note before heading back to the garage to check on the coroner's progress. The body had been lowered to a tarp on the garage floor, and Dr. Smith was closely inspecting the neck. Smith had worked in Mecklenburg County many years before moving north and becoming the Birch County coroner. Smith crossed paths often with Detective Baker during that time.

The detective bent down and peered over the shoulder of Dr. Smith. Deep, red lacerations were cut into the front of Baldwin's neck. Bloodstains trickled down his tee shirt, reaching his belt.

"How's it look, Doc?" Baker asked.

"I'll complete the autopsy to confirm it, but it doesn't look to me like this guy died from hanging."

"You can tell that by looking at his neck?"

"These lacerations are way too deep, and he was bleeding before he was hung over that railing. And look here," Dr. Smith said, pointing to the fingers of the corpse.

"His fingernails are broken and peeled back like he was fighting to pull the rope from his neck. He wouldn't have had time to do that if he hanged himself. His neck would've immediately snapped and his windpipe would've been crushed."

"So, what are you saying?" Baker asked.

"It looks to me like someone strangled him and then hung him over this railing. It shouldn't take long to confirm it once I get the body to my lab."

The CSI team spent six hours combing through the garage, every room in the house, and Lance Baldwin's car. They dusted for fingerprints and collected hair and lint samples, but they couldn't find anything pointing to who Lance Baldwin's partners might be.

- 13.2 -

IT WAS LATE AFTERNOON when Detectives Phillips and Baker returned to the Parsons Creek Police Department from the Lance Baldwin crime scene.

Beth and Ryan had spent the past six hours bouncing from the break room, to listening to the police band radio at the front desk, to watching cable news on the TV hanging from the ceiling of the visitors' center. They appeared more nervous than parents on prom night.

"Finally, maybe someone will tell us what's going on," Beth said, seeing Detectives Baker and Phillips enter the lobby.

Baker made eye contact with the couple and raised his hand as if to signal he needed another minute. It appeared he and Detective Phillips were engaged in a heated discussion.

Phillips waved his arms, scowling at Baker. At one point, he could be heard shouting, "No way!"

Baker was the calmer of the two, but more animated than usual. He put his hand on Phillips' shoulder. Ryan read his lips to say, "Be reasonable!" Phillips slapped Baker's hand away.

They finally parted, and Baker moved across the lobby toward Ryan and Beth.

"What was that all about?" Ryan asked.

"I'll tell you later," Baker replied.

"What did you find at Lance Baldwin's house?" Beth asked. "Any sign of Sarah?"

"You must keep what I tell you to yourselves, at least until the information is released to the public," Baker warned.

"Of course," Ryan replied.

"Lance Baldwin is dead. It appears his death was staged to look like a suicide, complete with a suicide note, but the coroner is convinced he was murdered."

"What did his note say?" Ryan asked.

"If Lance was murdered, I don't know how much of the note we can believe. It was likely written by his killer. The note confessed to kidnapping Heather McCoy and implied Lance played a role in her death. It also appears he was involved in a sex trafficking network."

"No mention of Sarah?" Ryan asked.

"No, but that doesn't mean Lance wasn't involved in some way. In fact, at this point, it seems likely."

"So, what's your theory on what happened?"

"We need to confirm it was Lance who bailed out Heather McCoy, but based on his description, I'm betting it was," Baker replied. "It appears whoever was working with Lance got spooked when Lance's photo started showing up everywhere. My guess is they decided to cut off Lance's trail back to them and set up the suicide note, with Lance taking the fall for the murder."

"What was your discussion with Detective Phillips all about?" Ryan asked.

"He's still convinced James Rigby is behind Sarah's disappearance. He's now insisting we keep the Heather McCoy case separate from Sarah's."

"Phillips doesn't think it's possible that Baldwin blackmailed Rigby?" Ryan asked. "He clearly could've learned about the hush money from Sarah."

"Sure, he thinks it's possible, but he has the clothing and blood evidence pointing to Rigby. More importantly, he wants to claim that both murders are now solved--one killer is in prison and the other is dead."

"What about Lance Baldwin's murderer? Whoever killed him is still on the loose," Beth argued.

"Killing young girls is sickening. It scares the hell out of everyone. But one sex trafficker killing another is less threatening to the public and not as urgent to solve," Baker explained.

"But that leaves Sarah hanging in the lurch. Phillips is assuming she's dead!" Beth shouted. "He's just serving his own interests."

"We'll keep looking for those responsible for killing Lance Baldwin," Baker said. "If there's a path to Sarah, we'll find it."

Officer Bronson came striding down the hall, eyes wide, waving at Detective Baker.

"Detective, you gotta see this," he said, holding out a ring of keys.

"What is it?" Baker asked.

"We found these at the Baldwin residence. I just matched one of the keys to Rigby's house and another to his SUV."

"So, it must've been Baldwin who planted the evidence," Baker said, "but how did he get access to Rigby's keys?"

"It doesn't take long to make copies. Maybe he took them at work before Rigby noticed," Bronson suggested.

"Sarah told me that Baldwin used to work nights parking cars as a valet," Ryan said. "That job provides a perfect opportunity to duplicate keys."

"This shoots a hole in Phillips' theory," Beth said. "Baldwin's killer is still out there, and whoever it is knows where to find Sarah."

- Day 14 -

CHIEF ADKINS ENTERED the conference room, sat, and cleared his throat. Those around the table looked up with tired eyes and haggard faces.

"Phillips, get us up to date. What's happened since yesterday afternoon?"

"Doc Smith confirmed Lance Baldwin was fatally strangled before being hung in the garage. Evidence at the crime scene is inconclusive in determining if one or more killers were involved.

"A ring of keys found inside the residence was later determined to contain keys to James Rigby's home and SUV, indicating that Lance Baldwin may have played a role in planting evidence."

"May have played a role?" Baker asked cynically. "You can bet once Rigby's lawyer learns of this, she'll be making a beeline to the DA's office demanding that murder charges be dropped."

"Okay. Okay," Adkins interrupted. "The point is that it appears Baldwin and whoever he was working with played a role in Sarah Campbell's disappearance. Go on, Phillips."

Phillips and Baker exchanged stares before he continued.

"Hair and lint samples taken from Baldwin's home and car are being matched against samples from Heather McCoy and Sarah Campbell. Results from the SBI lab are pending.

"Neighbors surrounding the crime scene were interviewed late yesterday. No one was able to identify anyone other than

Lance Baldwin coming or going to his home over the past several days.

"We contacted Sue Evans from Rolling Ridge and gained access to Lance Baldwin's work area. A search of his desk provided no leads to possible partners or other connections to sex traffickers."

Adkins leaned back and crossed his arms.

"Surely someone has seen this guy meeting with suspicious characters or with someone who could be connected to trafficking the girls," Adkins grumbled.

"So far, no one has," Phillips replied.

"Have we checked the Tennessee jail where the McCoy girl was last seen with Baldwin? Are we sure there were no other accomplices with him when he bailed her out?"

"I made a trip to Tennessee and met with the deputy on duty that night," Baker said. "I also talked with a witness who remembers seeing Baldwin lead the girls from the jail to his car. They both say Baldwin was alone."

"What about the other Tennessee and Kentucky county jails where we sent Baldwin's photo? Anything pop up yet?" Adkins asked.

"We have a possible hit in Victor County, a small jail in east Tennessee," Baker replied. "The sheriff thinks he recognizes him, and they're checking surveillance videos. I was headed there yesterday when I overheard the call to Baldwin's home."

"Well, there's still a killer on the loose, maybe more than one," Adkins said. "And with Baldwin's murder, the press is reenergized and as aggressive as ever."

The chief turned to Phillips.

"As of last night, the FBI assigned two additional agents to the trafficking case. They'll be here around noon. Get them anything they need and stay close to them."

Phillips leaned back and raked his hand over his face, releasing a slow exhale.

"Chief, wouldn't it be better if Baker updated the feds? He's closer to the McCoy case," Phillips argued.

"I talked to Detective Baker earlier, and we agreed it'd be best for him to stay engaged on the sex trafficking case. He'll let you know if and when he uncovers any leads."

Phillips shook his head and slumped forward in disgust.

"I'm headed to Victor County in a few minutes," Baker said. "I'll check back in this afternoon."

- 14.1 -

J.D. PACED IN HIS KITCHEN, chomping on a cigar butt that had extinguished an hour earlier.

"Murdered? He hanged himself, you morons!" he shouted at the TV on the counter.

Anger and fear welled inside him as he realized his plan had failed. He'd underestimated the coroner and the forensic skills of the SBI, but he was pretty sure Baldwin's house was clean. Nothing at the home pointed to him.

J.D. went to his office off the living room, pulled back the carpeting, and nervously unlocked the floor safe below. Inside were several small bags of pure white fentanyl, enough to kill the population of Parsons Creek several times over. Not wanting to waste any of his valuable stash, he selected the smallest bag from the safe and returned to the kitchen.

J.D. opened the cupboard and retrieved two cans of potato soup. He pulled the lids off the cans and poured them into a metal pot. He then unrolled the clear wrapping from around the fentanyl and placed it flat on the table, with the deadly powder atop the center of the wrapping. Retrieving a micro spatula that he used to calculate typical doses, he scooped four times from the white powder and dumped each into the soup.

"That should do it," he mumbled as he stirred the lethal concoction.

J.D. left the soup on the counter and went upstairs. He stepped down the upper hall to the first room on the left and pushed the door open.

Shari Yontz was unconscious, face down, on the bed. Her blonde hair lay tangled across her face. The breakfast tray he'd delivered earlier was on the nightstand. The eggs and juice had been consumed. Shari had passed out gripping a slice of toast in her left hand with a single bite taken.

J.D. padlocked the door from the outside and went downstairs, returning to the kitchen to retrieve the soup he'd prepared.

As he walked down the long lane to the cabin, crows heckled him from the treetops, seeming to understand J.D.'s intent.

He heard nothing inside as he unlocked the heavy door to the cellar. He pushed it open to find his prisoners side by side on the bed of insulation. Neither woman moved as he took a step inside.

"You girls dead?" he shouted.

Sarah was the first to raise her head. The fresh air coming down the stairwell hit her face, and she sat up. The man in the door was unmasked. She squinted, trying to focus on his face.

"I've seen you before," she mumbled, her voice raspy and low.

"You don't know me," J.D. snarled. "How's Jewell?"

Sarah shook the shoulder of the frail teen. Her eyes cracked open, and she turned her head toward the light.

"I'm hungry," Jewell squeaked with a tiny voice. "Is that food?"

"I guess you could call it that. Here. I want you to eat this before I leave," he said, sliding the pot toward Sarah.

She reached for the handle and pulled the soup to where Jewell was now sitting.

"I even brought spoons," J.D. said, holding out silver tablespoons.

"Why no mask?" Sarah asked. "And why the personal service?"

"He's gonna poison us!" Jewell called out. "Don't eat this!"

"You'd better damned well eat it!" J.D. shouted. "It might not kill you, but this will."

He pulled his silenced .45 from his belt and lowered it at the defenseless women.

"Eat!"

Sarah looked to Jewell. Stubbornness was etched on the teenager's face.

"Come on, Jewell. We don't have a choice," Sarah said.

Sarah ate the first spoonful, and then the second. Jewell reluctantly picked up her spoon and dipped it into the drug-laced potion.

With most of the soup remaining, Sarah began to lose control of her hands. Her arms fell limp and she dropped her spoon into the soup. Fumbling with her fingers, she was unable to retrieve the spoon from the pot.

"I can't eat any more," she mumbled. "I'm sick."

"Eat!" J.D. screamed. "There's more."

"Leave her alone, you fat prick," Jewell shouted, throwing her spoon and hitting him in his left eye.

J.D.'s nostrils flared as he leapt toward the women. Reaching back, he struck the barrel of the handgun against Jewell's temple. The blow opened a wide gash on the girl's forehead, spraying blood on Sarah and across the room.

Jewell's limp body fell against Sarah like a bag of wet sand. Sarah looked up at her captor with a dull stare, her cellmate across her lap.

J.D. kicked the pot, sending it hurling across the room. What soup remained splattered against the wall.

"If that doesn't kill you, I'll be back later to finish the job," he said before slamming the door and stomping up the stairs.

FALLEN from SIGHT

- 14.2 -

THE ROLLING HILLS surrounding Puget, Tennessee provided breathtaking vistas, but the closer Detective Baker got to the Victor County seat, the more focused he became. The landscape faded from his view.

He'd been told the corrections facility in Victor County was one of the toughest in the state. Hardened criminals and repeat offenders had passed through the jail on their way to maximum security prisons.

As he entered town, the well-maintained Puget streets and homes didn't reflect what he expected to find. He'd passed a new auto parts factory south of town, possibly explaining the middle-class prosperity.

Baker pulled his Chrysler sedan into the parking lot of the corrections facility before noon. He'd called ahead to make sure Sheriff Blake Winkler would be available on a Sunday.

Baker entered the lobby of the jail which was arranged surprisingly similar to the Brown County facility. He figured they all must have been constructed with the same state funding and guidelines.

A barrel-chested guard in uniform sat behind the counter reading a magazine. He tossed the periodical to the desk and stepped to the counter to greet Baker. The name in the slot of the on-duty sign read *Officer Jerry Winkler*.

"I'm Detective Baker with the North Carolina SBI. I'm looking for Sheriff Winkler. Any relation?"

"Yeah. He's my daddy's brother."

"So, that would make him your uncle?" Baker mocked.

"Yeah, that's right. What do ya want?"

"The sheriff told me he might have a video of a man suspected of trafficking girls out of the state," Baker replied. "I sent him this photo. He said it looked like the guy who bailed out a young woman just a few days ago."

The guard looked down at the photo on the counter.

"This is news to me. You'll need to talk to the sheriff. He's over at the courthouse in his office," he replied, pointing across the parking lot.

Baker stepped across the street and found the sheriff in his richly appointed office wearing street clothes. He was watching cable news on a wall-mounted TV, his feet propped up on his desk.

"Sheriff Winkler?" Baker asked through the open office door.

"That's right," he replied, dropping his feet to the floor.

"I'm Detective Baker. We spoke earlier."

The sheriff rose from his desk and turned off the television.

"You guys in Birch County sure have your hands full, don't ya?"

"Yeah, we're getting plenty of attention these days, but I've managed to keep my mug off TV," Baker replied.

"My staff was able to find the video of the guy in the photo you distributed. At least I think it's him. He was a cocky little prick. I came this close to locking him up," Winkler said, holding his forefinger and thumb an inch apart.

"Can I see it?"

"Sure. I have it loaded up right here, if I can figure out how to turn this thing on," he said, stepping toward a DVD player below the TV.

He double-checked to make sure the disc was inside and then hit *PLAY*.

The grainy video of a young man wearing a Carolina Panthers ball cap sitting in the lobby of the jail came on the screen. The man sat tapping his feet and checking his watch.

After a few minutes, a guard escorted a young blonde woman through the door leading to the cells. The man and the woman exchanged glances, but very few words, before walking out of the jail.

"Is that your guy?" the sheriff asked.

"There were only a few brief side views of his face, but it looks like Lance Baldwin. What do you know about Shari Yontz, the girl he bailed out?"

"Not much. It was her second drug offense. Her daddy, Marvin Yontz, lives about an hour north of here in Rocky Falls. That town's not much more than a hollow and a few shacks. I hunt up there, but I never met the man until your boy called him in to spring his daughter."

"The father knows Baldwin?" Baker asked, his voice rising.

"He seemed to know him, or at least knew of him. I got the feeling the daddy was making a few bucks on this transaction, but what could I do? He signed for his daughter. I had to release her."

"Do you have Yontz's phone number? I need to find out what he knows."

"No, but I'm sure one of my guys can find it and give him a call."

"Hurry! This could be the break we've been looking for."

- 14.3 -

BETH AND RYAN DROVE to Rolling Ridge, grabbing a quick lunch at Wendy's on the way. Ryan had called Sue Evans that morning, and she agreed to meet them at her office.

"We'd like to discuss Lance Baldwin. To get your thoughts on how this happened and what or who might have influenced him," he told her.

Sue was seated at her desk when they arrived. The office lobby was eerily quiet. In preparation for closing, signs, pictures, and all personal items had been packed. Even the lobby furniture had been removed. The room was an empty shell.

Chairs remained behind the two desks formerly occupied by Sarah Campbell and Lance Baldwin—one of them now dead, the other missing.

Sue's eyes were red, and her face drawn and tired-looking. She moved without energy.

"Thanks for coming in," Ryan said.

"I didn't sleep all night," Sue replied. "I was sad, shocked, and frightened, all at the same time. I still am."

"As you think back, is there anything at all that might have indicated Lance led a double life?" Ryan asked.

"I never suspected anything like this," Sue replied. "Not from Lance."

"Looking back now, knowing what he was capable of, were there people he met with who seemed out of place, or things he said that should've tipped you off?"

Sue was quiet. She looked down before focusing back on Beth and Ryan.

"I didn't want to say anything earlier. I didn't think it mattered, and I didn't want to initiate trouble."

"What is it?" Beth urged.

"Lance and Sarah were in a relationship together years ago, at least Lance thought it was a relationship. It was obvious he was fascinated by Sarah, maybe overly fascinated," Sue said.

"Did he ever hurt or threaten her?" Ryan bristled.

"No, I don't think so, but I did hear them arguing in the parking lot one night. I saw Sarah push him away, and then she jumped in her car and drove off," she continued. "Lance didn't come in the next day, and things were frigid around here for weeks, but it all seemed to pass."

"You should have mentioned this earlier," Ryan said, anger in his voice. "It's an obvious motive and explanation for Sarah's disappearance. What the hell were you thinking?"

"I guess I wasn't thinking," Sue replied, looking down. "But that was five years ago. Sarah's been with you for a long time. Everything seemed fine around here."

"So, Jeb Jones was right when he told us they were a couple. We should've listened more closely to him," Beth said. "Maybe he can shed some light on who Baldwin's been hanging around with."

"Yeah, if he'll talk to us," Ryan said. "We didn't exactly part ways in good company."

- 14.4 -

SHERIFF WINKLER'S deputy, Max Orton, burst into the sheriff's office. Detective Baker and the sheriff had been watching cable news as they waited.

"Sorry this is taking so long," Orton said. "I talked to Marvin Yontz's wife, but she says he won't come to the phone. He doesn't want to talk to no lawmen."

"Did you ask if she knew Lance Baldwin?" Baker asked, standing.

"She never heard of him," the deputy replied.

"Maybe if I talked to her," Winkler suggested.

"I don't think so. She said her husband is dead set on this."

"How long will it take to get to Rocky Falls?" Baker asked.

"Forty-five minutes if I have the lights flashing," the sheriff offered. "It might be fun to rip on over there."

BAKER HOPPED INTO the passenger side of the sheriff's Ford Taurus. He glanced at the odometer of the six-year-old vehicle as the sheriff hit the ignition. A total of 201,521 miles flashed below the speedometer.

"I hope these brakes and shocks have been replaced recently," Baker said.

"She rides as smooth as a buggy down a country lane," the sheriff replied, winking.

He accelerated to 80 mph as he blew past the *Welcome to Puget* sign at the edge of town. The shotgun affixed upright to the dash began to rattle as the car flew down County Road 182 toward the small Tennessee town.

Approaching a flashing yellow light intersection, the sheriff turned to Baker. "Hit the siren. I should keep both hands on the wheel."

Baker flipped the toggle marked *SIREN* and the Taurus flew through the crossroads in excess of 100 mph.

The two-lane road narrowed as they approached Rocky Falls. The welcome sign read *Population 250,* and the posted speed limit was 45 mph, which Baker hoped the sheriff would obey.

"I think his place is off Marsh Lane, just up here a bit," Winkler said.

A short distance further, the sheriff turned right down a dirt road marked with three deep tire ruts.

"Who gets the center rut when a car approaches?" Baker asked.

"Probably never happens," Winkler replied.

A half mile down the road was an opening in the trees with a lane leading to a weathered cabin. The small farm looked like the place Jed Clampett abandoned on his way to Beverly Hills.

A rusted garden tractor surrounded by weeds rested beside a barn. A sizable vegetable garden behind the cabin had yet to be plowed under for the winter.

Marvin Yontz lumbered onto the listing front porch in jeans and a grey sweatshirt as Baker and Winkler stepped from the cruiser.

"What's so damned important for two cops to come runnin' out to my place on the Sabbath?" he called to them.

"Mr. Yontz, we met several days ago when your daughter was released from my jail. This is Detective Baker from North Carolina. We're sorry to bother you on a Sunday, but you may have information that might help us locate a killer."

"I don't know no killers," Yontz replied belligerently. "You're wasting your time."

The tall mountain man turned and started to retreat back inside.

"Wait, this involves your daughter," Baker said. "She could be in serious trouble."

Mrs. Yontz hurried out the front door.

"My daughter?" she shrieked. "Have you seen Shari?"

"No, but we believe she may be with individuals responsible for killing a man. His name was Lance Baldwin. Your daughter was bailed out by him several days ago."

"Do you know about this?" she asked, turning to her husband with a lethal stare.

"I went down to get her out if that's what yer askin'," he replied.

"I thought you said she ran off after she was let out," his wife scolded. "You didn't say she left with some man."

"If your husband knows anything about Lance Baldwin or who might be associated with him, it could save lives, maybe even your daughter's," Baker said.

Mr. Yontz hovered a foot above his wife, but at that moment, he was the underdog in any fight that was to follow.

"You better tell these men what you know! And do it quick!" she shouted.

"Did the man who bailed out your daughter mention anyone he was working with?" Baker asked, taking a step forward.

"I don't know his name. He goes by J.D. Stocky fella."

"So you've met him before?" Baker asked.

"Yeah."

"How did you meet?"

"Don't wanna say here," Yontz said, glancing at his wife. "It was a private place. Anyway, we got talkin' and one thing led to another. He told me he had a good paying job for my daughter if things ever got tight. I called him after she got thrown in jail."

"You did what?" his wife screamed. "Did he pay you? Did you sell off your own daughter?"

"Someone's gotta support that screamin' kid in there," he argued.

"What else can you tell me about this J.D.? Where does he live? What does he do?" Baker asked.

"I'm not sure. I think he owns a business in North Carolina. I just know he worked with the Baldwin fella. He said he'd take good care of Shari."

"We need to run, but we'll let you know if we find your daughter," Baker said. "Pray that we do."

Baker and Winkler strode back to the car.

"I need to contact Detective Phillips in Parsons Creek. He's been working with me on this case. Give me a few minutes," Baker said.

Phillips picked up after three rings.

"We may have caught a break!" Baker exclaimed. "Does anyone around there know of a stocky man who goes by J.D.?"

"I don't, but I'll ask around. Who's J.D.?"

"He was working with Baldwin, and I just talked to a guy who said this J.D. fella paid to bail his daughter out of the Victor County jail."

"Shit. He's gotta be our guy!" Phillips shouted.

"Ask around," Baker said. "I'll do the same. Let me know what you find out."

- 14.5 -

DRIVING BACK TO Puget, Detective Baker called Ryan Nelson. He and Beth were in his Bronco when his cellphone rang.

"This is Ryan."

"It's Detective Baker. It sounds like you're driving."

"Yeah. Beth and I just left Jeb Jones' place. Didn't get much."

"Do me a favor and pull off the road for a minute," Baker said.

Ryan looked at Beth.

"Baker wants me to pull over."

The SUV coasted to a stop next to a roadside mailbox.

"What is it?" Ryan asked.

"I found someone who can identify a man who worked with Baldwin. He said a fella who goes by J.D. bailed his daughter out of jail a few days ago."

Ryan's head jerked back.

"Could he describe him?" Ryan asked.

"All he said was he was stocky and that he owned a business in North Carolina," Baker replied.

Ryan's eyes narrowed and his jaw tensed.

"What is it, Ryan? What's wrong?" Beth pleaded.

"I know where Sarah is," he said, handing the phone to Beth and whipping the Bronco around on the county road.

"Ryan, are you there?" Baker called into the phone.

"This is Beth. Ryan's driving like a madman. Said he knows where Sarah is."

"Call Parsons Creek PD now!" Baker screamed.

Ryan overheard the conversation.

"We're ten miles closer," he told Beth. "We'll get there first."

"He said we're closer," Beth told Baker.

"Tell me where he's going. I'll call Phillips," Baker said.

"Johnny Stratford's place," Ryan called out.

- 14.6 -

J.D. BURST THROUGH the cellar door. Jewell was contorted like a broken doll, with her head on Sarah's lap in a pool of congealed blood. Sarah was passed out, leaning against the damp prison wall. Neither of them moved.

The stocky killer stepped toward the women and placed two fingers to the side of Jewell's neck. He then checked for Sarah's pulse. Sarah groaned and her head moved slightly with the contact, but she quickly fell silent.

J.D. pulled his .45 from the back of his belt and lowered it at Sarah. He hesitated before stuffing the gun back into his belt.

"Too messy," he grumbled.

He then bent down and hoisted Jewell over his shoulder like a bag of cattle feed. Near death, she made no sound as he carried her up the stairs and laid her body in the bed of his pickup.

J.D. returned to the cellar for his second victim.

Sarah had lost twenty pounds during her two weeks of captivity. With little effort, the beefy kidnapper picked up the heavily sedated woman. Her ribs jabbed into his shoulder as he carried her to the truck.

He placed Sarah beside Jewell. Both were faceup as he covered their bodies with a heavy green tarp. He then tied the cover in place for the short trip he'd planned.

J.D. pulled the .45 from his belt and placed it in the center console of the pickup before starting the vehicle. As he pulled down the lane, he looked back at the makeshift prison.

What a shithole, he thought.

He turned back around to see the bright headlights of a Ford Bronco cutting through the early dusk and heading directly toward him.

The SUV slid to a stop fifty yards away, blocking J.D.'s exit with its headlights shining on the jet-black truck.

Raging with adrenaline, Ryan jumped out and strode to the front of his Bronco.

"Where's Sarah?" he yelled at the pickup.

Seeing Ryan unarmed, J.D. retrieved his .45 from the console and stuffed it in his belt behind him before stepping from the cab and facing Ryan.

"I don't know what you're talking about!" J.D. yelled back. "Save yourself a lot of trouble and just turn around and head outta here."

"I know you kidnapped Sarah, and I know you've been trafficking girls," Ryan called back. "The cops will be here in ten minutes."

J.D. looked back at his pickup. He thought for a brief moment before pulling the .45 from his belt. With both hands on the weapon, he aimed it at Ryan. J.D. squeezed off two shots as Ryan leapt behind a wheelbarrow at the side of the lane. The shots ricocheted off the gravel, missing Ryan by inches.

J.D. ran back inside his pickup as Ryan scrambled to his feet. Before the truck could accelerate down the lane, Ryan leapt forward and grabbed the handle on the driver side door, straining to pull it open.

With the .45 still in his hand, J.D. fired a single shot through the window, shattering it into a thousand pieces and hitting Ryan in the shoulder. Ryan released his hold on the door and fell like a rag doll to the gravel lane.

As Beth watched the horror before her, she remembered Ryan telling her about his .38. She scrambled to open the glovebox and found the handgun perched on top of the vehicle's owner's manual. With no time to think, she had to react.

J.D. stomped the accelerator and sped toward the SUV, sending dirt and gravel spewing into the air. Beth's eyes grew wide as a collision seemed eminent.

Suddenly, the pickup slowed to avoid nearby trees as J.D. attempted to maneuver past the bulky Bronco. At that moment, Beth grasped the gun with both hands and pointed it out the side window. Taking little time to aim, she fired three quick shots into the cab of J.D.'s pickup.

The truck veered to the right away from the SUV and slammed into a sturdy pine. Beth sat frozen with the gun on her lap, praying J.D. wouldn't emerge from the cab.

Ryan struggled to his feet and hobbled down the lane toward the collision. Beth leapt from the front seat and ran to meet him.

"Are you okay? I thought he killed you!" she cried, wrapping her arms around his waist.

A caravan of police cars careened off the highway and onto the gravel lane of the farmhouse. Beth and Ryan watched as each car slid to a stop in the front yard of the two-story home.

"Stratford's in the pickup. He has a gun!" Ryan called out.

Three officers approached the pickup in unison from wide angles. The officer on the driver's side was the first to reach the cab of the truck.

J.D. was slumped against the steering wheel, his eyes wide open, with a gunshot wound to his neck. The patrolman reached for a pulse and shook his head.

"Stratford's dead," he called out.

With the all clear, Phillips stepped to Ryan and Beth who were leaning against his Bronco.

"I don't know what to say other than that was the riskiest move any two people could ever make. You couldn't wait ten freaking minutes?" Phillips asked.

"Stratford was in a hurry to leave," Beth said. "If Ryan hadn't stopped him, he might've gotten away to do who knows what."

"Detective! It looks like we have bodies over here!" one of the officers announced.

Ryan's heart leapt to his throat as he ran toward the officer standing at the tailgate of J.D.'s pickup.

The two women were crammed against the cab. It was difficult to tell which arms and legs went with which body.

"Oh my God! It's Sarah!" Ryan called to Beth.

Forgetting his injury, Ryan jumped onto the bed of the truck, sat next to Sarah, and pulled her close with his good arm. She was so thin and pale, he barely recognized her. She didn't move or make a sound.

"Is she alive?" Beth cried.

Ryan leaned close to Sarah's face to feel her breath. As he pulled back, Sarah's eyes cracked open. He kissed her forehead, and her eyes closed.

"She's alive," Ryan announced, his voice cracking with joy.

"An ambulance is on the way," Phillips said. "Let Bronson and Smitgall take a look. They're medics."

The officers jumped onto the bed of the truck to administer aid. Smitgall pulled Jewell's limp body to the side and placed her on her back to check her pulse.

"I'm not getting anything!" he yelled before commencing CPR.

"China White," Sarah mumbled, lifting her head slightly. "He drugged us."

"They need Narcan! Now!" Bronson called, turning to Smitgall.

"We don't have any, but the ambulance will be here soon."

Smitgall repeatedly pressed the teen's slender ribcage with the palms of his hands, stopping briefly to listen for a breath.

A couple of minutes later, two ambulances arrived and the paramedics took over. After an injection of Narcan, Jewell's heartbeat returned, but she remained unconscious. She was quickly loaded onto the first ambulance and sped away to Watauga Medical Center in Boone.

Paramedics waited anxiously for Sarah to react to the lifesaving injection.

"How is she?" Ryan called out, being held back by Officer Bronson.

Suddenly, Sarah began to stir, her eyes cracking open. She was lifted from the truck bed onto a gurney and given IV fluids.

As she was about to be loaded into the second ambulance, Beth and Ryan hurried to her side. Ryan reached down and grasped her frail hand. Sarah opened her eyes, and for the first time, it was obvious she recognized Ryan and her sister.

"I made it," she said with a soft voice.

"You're gonna be fine," Beth said, reaching to her sister's shoulder.

FALLEN from SIGHT

The gurney was slid into the ambulance, and as Beth and Ryan watched silently, Sarah was whisked away.

"I can drive you and Beth to the hospital," Phillips told Ryan. "It's a thirty-minute trip. How's your shoulder? Do you think you can hang in there?"

"Sarah hung in there more than two weeks. I should be able to handle the drive to the hospital," Ryan replied with a smile.

- Conclusion -

SHARI YONTZ WAS THE ONLY person remaining in Stratford's farmhouse, and she was quickly treated by paramedics. Other than being extremely sluggish, she responded well to the Narcan injection and was in stable condition as she awaited transport to the hospital in Boone.

Detective Baker arrived as Parsons Creek PD was fully engaged in searching Johnny Stratford's farm. Baker was relieved to hear the Yontz girl was alive.

Shari was reclined at an angle atop a gurney, about to be loaded into an ambulance, when Baker stepped over to meet her.

"I'm Detective Baker. How're you feeling?"

"Like shit, but I've felt worse," Shari slurred.

"I talked to your father earlier today," Baker said. "If he hadn't cooperated, this could've ended much differently."

"My daddy? He don't care about me. All he cares about is huntin'."

"He and others will face charges for what they did, but your mom had no idea where you'd gone or what you were doing."

"I doubt that. She sticks up for him. She always believes his bullshit," Shari said, glaring at Baker before rotating her head away.

"I can read people pretty well, and your mom seemed very concerned."

"Why you tellin' me all this?" she asked, turning back to Baker. "What's it to you?"

"I'm tired of seeing young women, with their entire lives ahead, ruined by bad men and bad choices."

"Bad choices? What did you expect me to do?" Shari bristled. "Stay with my drunken father?"

"There are people who can help--safe houses, treatment centers. You don't need to run from one problem to another."

"You don't know me, or anything about my life," Shari protested, turning away again.

"You're right. I don't, but I can try to help," Baker replied. "After getting treatment, you'll be heading to a nearby safe house. If it's okay with you, I'm going to let your mom know where you'll be."

Shari's face softened as she thought.

"Could she bring my son to visit?"

"You can ask once you get settled, but I don't see why not."

IT WAS LATE MONDAY AFTERNOON as Beth and Ryan sat outside Sarah's hospital room, taking turns pacing the floor.

A nurse walked toward them from a station down the hall. "The doctor says you can go in now, but only for fifteen minutes."

Ryan pushed open the door with Beth at his side. They paused before entering. Sarah looked exhausted and emaciated, but removing two weeks of dirt, grime, and blood had dramatically improved her appearance.

"You look like Sarah again," Ryan said, stepping into the bright white surroundings.

"What happened to your arm?" Sarah asked, seeing Ryan's sling.

"Your crazy fiancé attacked an armed man," Beth said. "And guess what? He got shot."

"Shot?" Sarah exclaimed.

"Enough about me. I'll be fine," Ryan interrupted. "How are you?"

"He tried to kill us with a drug overdose," Sarah replied. "I'm gonna be okay, but I'm still feeling the aftershocks."

"How did this all begin?" Ryan asked. "Friday night we got engaged, and Saturday you disappeared."

"Lance found out about Rigby's hush money payments. I'd kept a diary of what I'd learned about the fake inspections, plus what I'd overheard from Rigby and the county inspector. The notebook disappeared, and I confronted Lance, but he said he didn't know anything about it."

"Why kidnap you?" Beth asked.

"He realized I was the only one who knew of the hush money. Once he decided to blackmail Rigby, he probably figured I'd squeal. Plus, he'd secretly hated me for years. I should have told someone about him."

"I thought you told me everything," Beth said.

"If Lance knew about Rigby bribing the county inspector, why did you keep it a secret?" Ryan asked.

"I was going to tell you. I just wanted to be one hundred percent sure. I was about to blow the whistle on my boss's boss, and I knew how you'd react. You'd have gone to the cops immediately."

"Next time, don't wait," Ryan said, bending down to kiss her cheek.

FALLEN from SIGHT

"There's not gonna be a next time," Sarah replied. "I'm going to take a break from real estate. Maybe find a retail job in Parsons Creek or Boone. Something with zero pressure."

"And discounts on shoes," Beth added, smiling as the nurse appeared in the doorway.

"Your time is up. This young lady needs lots of rest," she said. "And by the way, I just checked on the Anders girl. It looks like she's gonna make it."

Sarah's eyes glistened with tears.

"Jewell saved my life," she said, her voice quivering. "That evil bastard was forcing us to eat drug-laced soup when Jewell spoke up, hitting him in the eye with a spoon. She was pistol-whipped for her bravery, and I thought she was dead. Who knows where I'd be if she hadn't stepped in?"

"What do you think will happen to Jewell?" Beth asked. "So many of them go right back to that life."

"Them?" Sarah asked, frowning. "These girls are not that different from you or me. They just get trapped in a world they can't escape. Jewell will take advantage of this second chance. She won't go back."

"I hope you're right," Beth said.

"I know I am," Sarah replied firmly. "And as far as I'm concerned, we now have a second sister. If not for Jewell, I would've died in that rotten cell. I would've fallen from sight forever."

Please Provide a Review

Please let the author and other readers know what you think of *FALLEN from SIGHT* by going to Amazon.com and/or Goodreads.com and providing a rating and review.

Thank You

Acknowledgements

To those who have provided thoughtful feedback on prepublication copies of *FALLEN from SIGHT* and my other novels, I thank you.   Your comments and suggestions have been extremely valuable.

To my wife and editor, Claudia, thank you for your loving encouragement, patience, and constant enthusiasm.

About the Author

D.R. (Donn) Shoultz began writing fiction in the fall of 2010 following a sales and marketing career that took him around the world. His ongoing writing projects include posting regular thoughts to his blog, submitting short stories to competition, and working on his next suspense-filled mystery novel.

His crime and mystery novels feature a male and female protagonist you will get to know well, a criminal element you will despise, and a conclusion you will not see coming. In order of publication, his novels include:

Suspense/Crime Novels
- Corrupt Connection
- Better Late Than Ever
- Melting Sand
- Cyber One
- Gone Viral

Mountain Mysteries
- At the River's Edge
- Butcher Road
- Fallen from Sight

Donn's short stories are an eclectic collection of tales looking at the lives of lovers, schemers, everyday people and even pets. Each includes a twist and is designed to bring a tear and/or a smile to the reader. Several have received national contest recognition, including from *Writer's Digest* magazine. His short story collections include:

- It Goes On
- Most Men

Author profits from the sales of D.R. Shoultz's short story collections go to support North Carolina animal shelters.

You can learn more about D.R. Shoultz and his writing at http://DRShoultz.com

Made in the USA
Columbia, SC
10 January 2020